The Trouble with Pretty

Tara A. Iacobucci

Cover art by Tammie Trucchi

(inspired by Nicky Cao's photography)

For Owen, J.R., & Jane

I hope you never let another
(and that includes your mother)
decide what you should
and should not
love about yourselves.

The trouble with poetry
is that it encourages the writing of more poetry,
more guppies crowding the fish tank,
more baby rabbits
hopping out of their mothers into the dewy grass.

And how will it ever end?
Unless the day finally arrives
When we have compared everything in the world
to everything else in the world,

and there is nothing left to do
but quietly close our notebooks
and sit with our hands folded on our desks.

Billy Collins

Comparison is the thief of happiness.

Theodore Roosevelt

{ Prologue }

Words Have Power: Part I
By Aster Lamonte

I have often fantasized about living
free of mass
the love for myself
sanctified by weightlessness
unburdened by a number
projected on a scale
that at some point determined
not my health but my worth

Before I learned the rules,
that scale was nothing but a toy
at the doctor's office,
a fun numbers game to pass the time.
When the nurse left the room,
after recording the number
in some official medical notebook,
I squatted, lifted, and jumped,

prompting the number to change.
My feet bare, laughing,
watching the tiny red pointer
swinging back-and-forth before finally resting
on an exact digit
I had no presumption that this number
would someday soon,
inevitably and unceremoniously,
measure my value.

When did the change occur exactly?
When did I give this seemingly innocuous number
so much power?

When did I let it stop me
from exposing my body
to those sunny skies
and vulnerable to the ocean's ripples?
When did I start covering every inch of my skin
instead of introducing it to the waves
that I wished upon
begging for the smallness of this number
so I could love myself more?

For me, I guess the change came
after a little lifetime of words
disguised disgust woven between them
like coiled string
and spoken without much thought
but those words became pitchforks
that unearthed
all of my buried insecurities:
the script etched on bathroom walls

and whispered in school bus lines
or spewed like bile from the mouth
of the only person
who was supposed to see me as perfectly beautiful

Words have power
they took up residence in my thoughts
forming shadows
they walked around with a pompous freedom
shutting down any lights
that sheltered compassion reserved
for weak moments

I believed the scale could free me
of this internment
like a certain number might convince me
that I was worthy

Instead
the scale became my personal demon
hiding underneath my bed
and each morning
after it reviled me
I blamed only myself
in hopes this morning ritual could change me
for more punishment,
I collected glossy pictures
the paper, tissue thin,
would crumple with only a delicate, closed fist
and become unrecognizable balls of shiny color.
Wishing that the concept of beauty
held immeasurable in those pictures
was just as easily ruined

I put tape on the backs of each,
covered my mirror and bedroom walls.

My mom approved,
those pictures meant *motivation*

and Dad said nothing
when I took down
the Disney princesses
and replaced them with the others
thinking *that must be what girls do.*

For a long time,
I couldn't see my reflection
in the mirror
covered with these flawless women
I tore out of magazines.

{ SUMMER }

1

I know that rumors can start from all sorts of foolish places, like a joke, or a miscommunication, or a white lie even. I know that rumors are often not true. And so I keep pushing away the fact that most rumors usually start from some sort of truth.

Because the rumor I heard last night, that my boyfriend has been cheating on me, must be a lie. Because Adam could not possibly be that cruel, and I couldn't possibly be that stupid.

I just want to be alone, but Dad comes home from work early to watch the continuing news coverage for the Democratic Convention and Hillary Clinton's acceptance speech, and he wants me to watch with him because it is "historic." I've pretty much been in the fetal position on the couch since this morning trying to calm my nerves, figuring if I just stayed still then maybe everything would be okay.

Dad throws his lunch box and tool belt on the kitchen counter and then sits down without showering even though his clothes and hands are smudged with sheetrock dust. "I want you to see this," he tells me when I ask him if he's even going to at least remove his heavy work boots. "C'mon."

"Do I really need to?" I whine. "I mean, I can't even vote yet." It's not that I'm against hanging out with Dad, it's just that I'm a little distracted by the fact that, if the rumor is true or if I can't prove that it's false, my life will be a complete disaster.

"Yes, you have to," Dad says, sitting at the edge of the couch, holding the TV remote. "If you have a daughter someday, she will not even appreciate that a woman could be the U.S. President because that's all she will know. But, you can tell her that you were there, that you were part of history." He says this as he pats the seat beside him.

To be honest, I never really cared much about any politics until I saw that a woman might actually be our next president and I thought it would maybe be cool to see a woman with that much say in our world. Dad, a loyal Democrat, noticed my curiosity and has been trying to engage me in all sorts of political discussions and experiences ever since. It's just that lately, every time I turn on the TV or scroll through social media, I'm a little turned off by the amount of criticism about her appearance, her obsession with power and money, and the unnecessary rehashing of her husband's sexual misconduct. I haven't seen much coverage on the actual issues either, the ones that Dad is constantly ranting about, like healthcare and the economy, so I don't exactly know what I'm supposed to be learning. It seems like I'm watching a bad reality TV show which makes sense since Donald Trump is the star.

"Fine," I say and sigh, taking a seat next to Dad.

I look again at my last text from my best friend, Leah. *No news yet. Don't worry--I'm getting to the bottom of this. Heading straight to the source.* The source, I think, must be Liz, the girl in question. Apparently, Liz told someone that she and Adam had been hooking up. And that someone told someone. And so on. Until eventually a girl named Bridget who I hardly know got stinking drunk at the party I was at last night, walked up to me and blurted, "You don't even know, do you?"

"Know what?" I said, annoyed and caught off guard.

"That Adam's been cheating on you." She looked at me with such pity that I had to look away. "With Liz," she added. And then she ran to the nearest bathroom and vomited.

Afterwards, when I completely broke down on the ride home, Leah brushed it off and said there's no way we could listen to that nuisance of a girl who can't even control her alcohol, but I couldn't let it go. "What if it *is* true. I mean, I've always been suspicious of him and Liz."

"You know I don't like Adam and think you should have dumped his ass months ago," she said. "But I just don't think he's stupid enough to cheat. Especially with loudmouth Liz."

I left voicemails and texted Adam about it last night but didn't get an answer. I mean, it's a little weird that I haven't heard from him, but his parents pack his schedule so he's probably exhausted. Or maybe they took his phone again; he's always pissing them off. When I continued to rage and hyperventilate this morning, Leah told me that she'd take care of it.

Now, to take my mind off of it, I try to pay attention to the speeches because I know they're important, or should be important, to me. But I'm too distracted by my phone which must be broken or something because not one text is coming through-- not from Adam or Leah.

"Dad, can you call my phone?" I ask. "I want to make sure it's working."

Dad's falling asleep beside me despite his excitement over this historic moment. It doesn't help that he gets up at 4 a.m. to go to work every day and then he has been staying up past midnight to catch the news. He opens one eye and peers at me. "Um, no. Busy."

I turn my phone off and turn it back on again. Then, I text Leah asking if there's any new information. *Relax man! I'll text you as soon as I get some answers.*

Mom comes home and stands behind us and I can't see her, but I bet her hands are on her hips and she's glaring at the mess Dad left on the counter, taking slow breaths, trying to decide if she should just clean it up herself.

"Hey Mom," I say.

"Hey guys," she says and my dad nods in her direction.

As a response, she heads towards the kitchen and I can hear her loudly putting Dad's stuff away. She comes back a few minutes later and asks if we've had dinner. Dad's fully asleep on the couch now, snoring gently, and so I answer no for both of us.

"I'll make us something," she says but then sits on the couch across from me. "What are you watching?"

"Dad's making me watch stuff about the Convention," I say and roll my eyes. We watch the TV for a while. I think about talking to her about the rumor since I tell her practically everything. Well, at least as much as a teenage daughter can and should tell. But why bother telling her this drama if it's not even true?

Hillary has finally taken the stage and has on all white from head to toe. I guess she decided to take one color from our country's flag and then really go all out with it.

"Oh God, did she get fat?" my mother asks but it's more of a statement. "I mean, what is that woman wearing? She looks like a hideous, shapeless cloud."

Of course Mom would comment on Hillary's appearance and forget about the historical relevance. In Mom's eyes, beauty should be every women's top priority. Even though Mom's a top person at her company and makes more money than Dad, she still would rather be beautiful than anything else. And she is a knockout. Honestly, if Mom ran for president, or anything for that matter, she'd win *because* of her looks. I guess Hillary has to work a lot harder at getting votes.

To me, Hillary's white suit is a new start and maybe she wanted to divert people's attention from her looks since this is the presidency, not a beauty pageant. Then again, maybe Mom's right.

"I wonder if her stylist was hoping the white would purify her of all of those rumors about her husband's affairs," Mom says.

"Seriously," I say and try to laugh.

It just doesn't seem so funny--all the jokes about her. All I ever seem to hear about is the story of Bill Clinton and his Impeachment trial that so infamously involved the affair he had with his secretary. Even though the Senate acquitted him of all charges, it's like this is the only thing people think about when they look at Hillary Clinton. And I know the rumors that surround her too; how she paid off or possibly attacked the women who accused her husband. I don't know, the truth is always muddy, right? Dad always says that we should separate public figures and the work they do from their personal lives, and that even Martin Luther King, Jr. supposedly had affairs with prostitutes, but I don't know. I'm just amazed at how Hillary put that shame behind her and stepped forward onto the stage, especially in that white suit that, let's face it, isn't fixing anything.

I wake up Dad so that he doesn't miss her speech. Mom lets us eat our dinner on the couch and then she disappears to her room. Hillary's speech is mostly about how Trump wants to divide us, and how we need to work together to make change. Most of her hope for these changes rests in the young people. "We have the most tolerant and generous young people we've ever had," she says, and I wonder if that's true. Because I go to school with "young people" and, well, some of them are the most intolerant people I know. After that, I tune her out; I'm still waiting for my phone to buzz anyways.

By midnight, it's official. Hillary Clinton becomes the first woman in history to accept the nomination to run for president of the United States, and, exhausted, I momentarily forget about Adam and fall asleep thinking of crumbling walls and broken glass, but the peace and hope of this historic moment is brutally shattered after Leah wakes me up the next morning to confirm the news that the rumors are true.

*   *   *   *

"I'm so sorry Star," Leah says, but I know she really wants to say, "I told you he was a snake."

"How did you find out?" I ask.

"Liz has terrible friends who love to gossip. One of them even had pictures from Liz. I'm coming over now."

"I really just want to be alone. I'll call you later."

I hang up and cry softly in my room, the humiliation feeling like hot flames sparking all around me until my mind remembers Hillary. Now, it's easy to understand the degradation she must have felt all those years ago when Bill shouted proven lies about his mistress, and her private life became a public spectacle. My own humiliation will surely become fodder for high school gossip. My only hope is that the freshness of it will not last until the fall.

Eventually, my mother knocks gently, tissues in hand; she must have heard me crying. "Oh, Aster. What's wrong?" Her face is all concern and love as she sits beside me on my bed, and I surrender to her strong arms, willing myself to survive the first sting of shame. I breathe in her familiar, vanilla scent as she lets me cry. When my tears finally pause, and I can choke out the awful truth of my first real relationship, she asks, "Do you want my advice?" And of course I do. My mother. I long for her beauty, her tulip lips and bright eyes, her perfectly angular face and petite frame. In her early forties, she looks more like my sister than my mother, and people just meeting her never fail to point this out. I don't think she will ever age; even in white, she could never be a shapeless cloud.

She says, "If you just lose fifteen pounds, maybe a new hair style, some new clothes, this boy who hurt you will suffer. Because when he sees you, he'll regret everything."

It is the first time she tells me, explicitly, that how I look is unacceptable, and that there are consequences. If Hillary had paid more attention to her appearance instead of becoming "haggard" and "fat" as the media and even my mother point out, would her husband have so easily had those affairs?

Did she make it easier to cheat by paying too much attention to her own success?

I search my mother's eyes, weighing her words. I know they must come from love, but the impact of them feels similar to the pain I feel from the news of my boyfriend's duplicity. "Okay, ya Mom." She hands me another tissue; I sniffle. She's watching me carefully, a small smile of satisfaction on her face because she believes her advice will save me.

"I will help you, honey," she says now, squeezing my hand gently. "It will be the summer of pretty. Trust me. I will transform you so that Adam will beg for you to take him back. Okay?"

Her offer sounds like a magical gift that does not exist, but I accept it anyway, envious of that little bit of hope flickering in my mother's eyes; I let it in, just like always. "Okay, mom."

"Let's start now," she says, jumping up. "You want to go for a run down to the water before I go to work? Burn some calories?"

There's a small beach just down the street, and this week's heat wave has increased its popularity, bringing in many tourists but also residents of my town. Outside of my window, I can see the green and rolling mountains in the distance, the sun hot and bright in the sky, but I would rather not feel that heat today. Even getting out of bed sounds like too much of an impossibility.

"Can we start tomorrow?"

"Sure," she says and tucks my hair behind my ear. "I'll order us some healthy lunch later and we can talk then."

"I really don't think I'll be hungry."

"Well, maybe that will help kickstart your weight loss," she says and I'm shocked to hear a note of glee in her voice. She pats my hand and tells me she loves me. I bet she'd love me more if I were thin.

As she gets up to leave, the lump in my throat makes it hard to talk without crying, but I don't want to start up again since it might make my mom stay even longer, so I stay silent, swallowing. Of course I knew she'd in some way talk about my appearance, but I didn't anticipate that it was possible for my shame to deepen and bury itself into my core.

Because even though she always reiterates this same advice about the importance of appearances, it is in this crucial moment that I begin to believe that if only I was thin and pretty, bad things would not happen.

*　　　*　　　*　　　*

When my mom leaves, the promise of her fixing everything finalized with the close of my door, I consider calling Adam again, expecting him to deny everything or at least beg for a second chance. Would I give him one, like Hillary gave Bill? Would that be brave or pathetic?

I sit in my dark room, shades drawn, wondering what comforting words Hillary received after realizing the truth. Did someone make her question her looks, despite her own power and steadiness?

Minutes later, I receive a text from Adam: *I'm sorry if I hurt you. It just sort of happened, me and Liz. We are together now. Please don't respond. I don't think I could take you hating me. Let's talk in a couple of months. When emotions aren't so high. I'll explain everything*

Typical Adam. Lots of statements, no need for a response. Always in control. It takes all my strength not to respond. I picture Liz--straight black hair, petite but muscular, always alive with a loud laugh and aggressive opinions--and it's like I've been punched; I close my eyes to block out the sensation, but all I can see are the two of them together. And the images seem so real because I had seen them together with my own eyes, but I just stupidly believed Adam when he told me they were just friends. When he told me to be cool, to stop being jealous, to trust him. I had felt like *I* was the one ruining the relationship.

I sit on my bed, rocking myself, wishing I could talk to someone who might understand. I can't talk to

Leah because I already know what she will say.
That he's a snake. That he could never be trusted.
That he didn't treat me right.

I can't talk to Dad either since he's not the easiest
person to talk to. Dad does not love words. He
signs his cards "From Dad." He nods instead of
saying "yes." His most common responses are
"Uh-huh" and "hmmm" so that he doesn't even
need to open his mouth. He only willingly talks
about two topics: sports and politics. If someone
broaches another topic with him, Dad will respond
with sarcasm, a decoy so that all conversations not
related to his passions will flounder.

And then there's, or there's not, my brother, Luke.
His empty bedroom is just down the hall; he doesn't
live here anymore, now that he's going into his final
year of college. Not that he ever really did. I mean,
he *lived* and slept and ate dinner here but it's like I
never really knew who he was. He barely talked to
me besides a nod here and there and a "leave me
alone" if I ever went into his room. So, ya, he's not
someone I would call during one of my lowest
moments.

Since I'm alone, I can't help falling deeper into an
unfamiliar agony. I climb under my covers wanting
to hide my entire body, the one he rejected. The
one my own mother cannot even accept. Why am I
so fat even though I'm always on a diet? How
come I eat less than Leah, who scarfs down carbs at
every meal and drinks chocolate milk for breakfast,

yet she has a model's body and I am always a little overweight says my doctor at every physical?

I know I should get up and do something about my sadness, gain control, that's what my mom would tell me to do, but instead I roll over, pull the blankets over my head and pretend sleep is feasible. But when I close my eyes, all I can see are Hillary's ugly pant suits and thin-lipped smile.

*　　　　*　　　　*　　　　*

Mom drags me out of bed the next morning on a mission to recreate me in order to show Adam what he is missing. I dread clothes shopping and have avoided the confrontation I will inevitably have with the mirror, but I need new school clothes since my last year's pants no longer fit, though I lie and tell Mom they are no longer in style.

Mom and I go to lunch first so she can interrogate me about the ugly parts of myself before she makes me over. I look at the menu and my mouth waters for a burger and fries but I know Mom won't approve.

"I'll have a salad with grilled chicken and water," I tell the waitress.

"Dressing on the side!" Mom chirps at both me and the waitress. "And I'll have the same."

When the waitress leaves, Mom explains, "You

should always get the dressing on the side, honey. That way, you can just dip your food instead of smothering it in fat."

I grind my teeth. "Okay, mom."

We sit in silence, drinking our water. "I'm thinking you should go blond," Mom suddenly says, sounding excited. "Remember when you were younger and had blond hair. That really made those green eyes of yours shine. What do you think? Do you want me to make an appointment with my hairdresser before you go back to school?"

I can't stand Mom's snobby hair salon, filled with rich women who would just *die* if even a strand of gray showed therefore committing to pay a hundred dollars every month to color over it. But I know Mom has resolved to improve me so I acquiesce. "Sure, but can I bring Leah?"

Mom loses her smile. "You don't want me to come with you?"

"No, it's not that. I just think Leah might want to do something different to her hair too. Maybe you could make two appointments?"

"Oh, ya, sure. But Leah's hair is so pretty--that natural curl she has. I hope she doesn't change it too much. Plus, with her dark skin, it wouldn't make sense for her to change the color."

"Yea, I know Leah is perfect," I say, trying not to sound wounded, "but maybe she could just get a trim."

"Okay, I'll make you two an appointment for next week. The boys will not be able to resist you!"

After our bland lunch, Mom drives me to the mall. The stores for my age pump out loud music and the smell of potent cologne wafts out to the lobby. When we walk in, the pictures of perfectly toned bodies loom above our heads like omnipotent Gods. I trail my fingers along pretty silk and cotton tops and finally pick out some dark-colored ones that might flatter my figure by hiding it. The bottom half of me is harder to conceal. I grab some pants at the bottom of the pile and rush into the dressing room before Mom notices the size.

Even though they are the largest ones in the store, the pants are too tight, as usual, but I try anyways to zip them over impossible hips.

Mom knocks lightly, "Can I see?"

She is always gracious, will buy me anything I ask for, and I am grateful, so I pull the shirt down low and open the door.

When she stands beside me, I avoid our reflections.

I do not look like her.

I do not have her petite frame or her tanned, flawless skin. While she has model features--dark green eyes, perfectly straight nose and teeth, plump lips--I am, at best, just ordinary.

Mom does her best, twists her lipsticked lips up, mimicking a smile, while assessing my body so closely that I wrap my arms around my middle. "Let's keep looking," she says, and, staring at my reflection, bites hard on her lower lip and her nose pulses like it's been assaulted by a bad smell. But I hope, still, for words of compassion. Maybe I don't look as bad as I think?

"You looked so good when you lost weight, Aster. What happened?" she says.

Why do I always believe that she will comfort me in my most vulnerable moments since her words are destined to unearth all of my buried insecurities?

"Not sure," I mumble and put my hand on the door to close it.

I wish I could soften
her stone cold words
or smooth them down
and skate on them like ice

So that when she speaks with gravel
I could remember
how, years ago, she accidentally
slammed my fingers in her locked car door
then dumped the entire contents
of her pocketbook out on the sidewalk
and then
coming undone
hysterically searched for her keys
as I howled in agony

And when she finally managed to open the door
her words were like silk
in my ear
that dulled the throbbing
in my fingers

And I could remember
those nights of satin
as she lay beside me, past my bedtime
giving in to my demands
for one more story
of her happily ever after
tucked me in
with a hushed lullaby
her voice a whisper,
gentle as that tiny pause
at the end of a line of poetry

2

One of my parent's wedding photos, which hangs in our living room, shows an absolutely gorgeous couple. My mother, always a beauty, has her head thrown back, mouth wide open, laughing. My dad looks tanned and flawless in his black tux with olive green eyes and a full head of Tom Cruise hair. He stares at my mother with so much heartbreaking affection that it makes me uncomfortable sometimes when I look at it, especially because of the present, how my father descended to our basement to avoid my mother who, despite the years, became a radiant sun, always a distance too far to reach. Growing up, they had seemed invincible, armed with endless love; now, she glares at him across the dinner table when he chews too loud, and he no longer offers to hold her hand or rub her feet at night.

Time treated them both differently and they aged in opposite ways, like the Obamas during their eight years in the White House. My mom, thanks to an obsessive monthly skin and hair treatment, daily workouts, and a committed diet (I didn't say it was easy) saved her youth from expiring. She thrived in her busy, corporate life, entertaining people with her charisma, getting raises and higher positions every few years.

Dad had started working construction at age 19. After going to college for a year in an attempt to please his parents and play out a football scholarship, he slowly drifted away from the classroom in the spring to help his uncle build a house. While in a classroom he felt trapped, useless; nothing really happened in the lectures he heard and the notes he took: yet, daily while building this house he saw its progress, a real structure taking shape because of his own two hands. At the end of the summer, Dad dropped out of school and joined his uncle's construction company. My dad, although he loves his job as a general contractor, grew tired. His skin suffered from too many days working in the sun and his hair thinned. His body, once athletic and built for speed on the football field, now looked worn down, aged.

I don't think my dad was jealous, but he must have hated the way other men looked at my mother. One time, at a party for my mom's work, one of her coworkers, after meeting my dad for the first time, jokingly asked my dad how he got someone so good looking. My dad's best friend from high school repeatedly says, even though my parents are the same age, "How'd you get such a young wife?" My mom's success at work and her youthful good looks seemed to create a rift between them. My brother, Luke, and I never heard them fight but we of course noticed the obvious signs that their marriage no longer looked like it did in that photograph. So I was not surprised when, the night after my brother left for college, my dad began sleeping in my brother's room and my mom locked her bedroom door.

*   *   *   *

Since my parents avoid talking to each other at all costs, Mom comes back from her Sunday run with lunch, and asks me if I'd tell him it's on the table for him when he's ready. Even though they barely talk, they remain committed to obligatory marriage tasks, just to keep up the façade. I'm happy for the excuse to go talk to Dad since it's nearly the end of summer and I've barely seen him.

I find Dad in the garage, his little workshop, where he keeps his tools. He is adding a bathroom to the basement so that Luke will have one when if he ever comes home to stay (which is doubtful). I think Dad must feel bad for moving into Luke's room forcing Luke to stay in the spare room in our dark basement.

"What's up?" I say, crossing my arms over my chest and standing awkwardly between piles of mess. "Mom got you lunch. It's in the kitchen."

Dad nods his head in my direction, a sign he's heard me. He's got his measuring tape out, fat pencil behind his ear. He kneels down to fit two pieces of tubing together. Over the years, Dad has taught himself electrical and plumbing work. I swear he could build and finish an entire house all by himself.

I'm not sure why I stay and attempt a conversation with him, but I know that I love his calmness, his level head and sense of humor. I'm also hoping he'll ask me to help him with this project, like he used to do when I was little. He'd give me pathetic jobs and I'd feel important. Like holding his nails or shining a light into a darkened cabinet. It seems that when I started dating Adam, he no longer needed my help.

"Did you hear our girl Hillary's up in the polls?" Dad finally says, at last discomforted by my obvious silence.

"Ya, good news," I say, but I don't want to talk about Hillary or politics. So, instead, to distract Dad, I blurt out, "Adam and I broke up."

Dad doesn't miss a beat. "Oh well, good riddance. Next time you get a boyfriend can you make sure he likes football? That kid doesn't even know who Bill Belichick is."

I smile, remembering how Adam came over for dinner once, looking completely puzzled when Dad began discussing the NFL's charges against Tom Brady. The conversation soon fizzled out when Adam explained that he didn't follow sports, which was completely sacrilegious in my dad's eyes.

Dad's not looking at me; he's caught up with his

fixtures or maybe he's just avoiding my gaze. "Can you grab me that glue?" he asks.

I grab it but don't hand it to him yet. "Dad, am I ugly?" I ask, picking some dried glue off the top.

"You? Yea, you're hideous. When the doctor first showed you to me, I was like 'yikes put that ugly thing back!' But he wouldn't. So we got stuck with you."

"Daaad," I groan. "Can you ever just answer a question?"

"Okay fine, but I need your help first. Can you hold these two pieces together so that I can attach them with that glue." He holds out two tubes.

"Sure," I say and put my hands out for the parts, even though I know this is a one man job.

In the mornings

before the sun speaks to the sky
Dad nestles his coffee into the cup holder
and drives into the city
toolbox clinking in the backseat

I am a little girl
awakened by the familiar opening sound
of the garage
and I can't fall back asleep
I am out of bed
with my own toolbox
overflowing with words
I have to sit on it
to close it tight
By mid-afternoon
there is ink under my nails
rhythms and patterns mottle my shirt
and my fingers ache
from verse
just as Dad comes home
dirt under his nails
dust on his clothes
legs aching
from shaky lifts and ladders

he nods in my general direction
his "hello", his "i missed you"

Thankfully we have building in common

3

Now, the first thing I do when I wake up in the mornings (even though I barely sleep) is think about Adam. I want him to be the furthest thing from my mind, I want to stop thinking it will be him every time my phone beeps, I want to stop picturing him when I close my eyes. It seems like every waking moment is spent thinking about how to forget him, or thinking about how I can win him back, even though I know deep down, that he was never any good.

It doesn't help that my summer job at Tops Café ended early for renovations and Leah works almost every day at a local daycare. I spend most of my days alone, walking through my house like a zombie, dodging the check-up phone calls from my mother.

I turn on the TV, programmed to the local news, probably by my father this morning before he left for work. Hillary's the top story, as usual. It's either her or Donald Trump. People still hate her...no surprise there.

The news desk is currently discussing if Americans can take gender out of the equation when we cast our votes or are we, in some way, voting for the sex we believe can lead our country. One male anchor says he does not have a bias against women when voting. For instance, he explains, he voted for a woman last year for school committee, then he laughs at his absurd joke and makes everyone at the table uncomfortable.

A female anchor says she believes, nowadays, because of how *forward* our country is, that we cannot argue that sexism will play a major role in this election. "People don't hate Hillary because she's a woman," she explains patiently. "People hate her because she lies."

If it's not about Hillary's sex, then why do I see t-shirts with her face, and hear chants at Trump rallies, that say things like, "Trump that Bitch," or "Life's a Bitch, let's not elect one," and "Hillary SUCKS (but not as good as Monica)." Why the word Bitch? Why a word that is only derogatory toward women? And why a reference to her husband's affair with the not-so-subtle point that, if she could have pleased Bill sexually, then maybe he wouldn't have cheated on her?

More people chime in on the panel, saying they agree, that they would vote for a woman if they respected her and it's just that Hillary has lost all of their respect. Agitated, I take out my phone and do a Google search. "What do anti-Trump shirts say?" Of course, they are mean-spirited. Many liken him to Hitler. One says, "Dump Trump." Another, "If Trump Wins, I'm Moving to Canada." But, nothing about his maleness. Nothing that puts down men. Nothing that *actually* questions his right to run for president.

If Hillary were a man, would the hate for her feel so violent?

I turn the station, feeling something unsettling deep in my bones, and eventually I drift off listening to angry voices discuss corrupt politicians.

* * * *

Mom calls around noon. "How are you holding up?" she asks.

I rub sleep from my eyes. "I'm okay. Still not sleeping. Still feel miserable."

"Why don't you go for a run?" she suggests. Exercise is her solution for any emotional ailment. Or a healthy, extra dose of vegetables.

"Ya, I will after lunch," I say, even though it's the last thing I want to do.

"Okay, see you when I get home. Tell Dad to start dinner, okay? I won't be home until late. And Aster?"

"Ya Mom?" I yawn.

"You're not going to win anyone's affections by sitting around on your ass all day and moping."

* * * *

Some days, I think I might be okay, at least enough to show my face at school in two weeks even though everyone most likely knows what happened.

Damn social media. Adam posts pictures on his Instagram at least twice a day of him and Liz. Last week, they took a trip to the Lakes region in New Hampshire; this week, they are vacationing in the Cape together with her parents. I wonder if she has to pretend that he's a drumming God like I did. Adam, if anything, enjoys having his ego stroked.

I'm lying on my bed, absentmindedly looking through social media when I hear the front door open and close and then someone yells, "Hello?" Leah. She must have the day off. I know she's my best friend and she only has my best interest at heart but I'm not in the mood. Leah has no idea what it's like to feel this sort of heartbreak, her beauty acting as an impenetrable shield.

I stay quiet, hoping she'll get the hint, but eventually she lets herself in and I can hear her coming up the stairs. Then, a knock on my door. She will only become louder the more I try to shut her out. "Come in," I say, quietly.

When she comes in my room, she wastes no time and opens up my blinds. She sits next to me on my bed and takes my phone. "I told you to stay off the media," she says.

"I know," I say meekly. "I have a problem."

"What's that asshole bragging about now?" She starts browsing through my phone.

"They're at a hotel right on the beach. Liz takes selfies of them every five minutes and posts them to both of her accounts," I whine and bury my face in my pillow.

"Gag," she says then stops on a picture of the two of them. "He's complete scum. He looks like a vampire, you know. Like, has he ever seen the sun?"

"I don't even want to look at him. You're going to have to kidnap my phone so I can stop obsessing."

"Yup...so what are we doing this weekend, now that we aren't going to be looking at Adam's ugly mug?" She tosses my phone on the bed as she stands up and tries to look in my full length mirror. "Fuck Star, I can't even see myself!" she complains. She reaches up and lifts up one of the pictures I've got taped there.

"No, don't," I say, standing up. "Those are for...something." I suddenly realize how stupid it all must look.

"Helping you what?" Leah scoffs, "Learn how to look dependent and vulnerable?" She points to a woman who is looking away from the camera, gingerly biting her pointer finger. You can see the tip of her tongue, pink and suggestive. "This is what you want to be like?"

"No, it's just...not a big deal."

"Well it's just unhealthy. You know they're all Photoshopped right? Like this-" she points to a woman in a tiny bikini, "doesn't actually exist."

Funny. Because Leah is a mirror image of the same woman, just a more voluptuous, sexy version. Like J-Lo but more flawless, if that's even possible. "That's easy for you to say, Leah. You-" I cup my hands and gesture at her, trying not to sound annoyed. "Look at you." I know it's not Leah's fault, but she has no idea what it's like to live in my body, no idea what it's like putting on clothes that you constantly have to adjust, check in the mirror, stretch out. She can put on anything and it fits like a second set of skin. It's easy for her to criticize me for wanting what she already has.

"I'm not perfect, Star," she answers, crossing her arms. "And why are you always so fucking obedient?" she yells, her hands now wild, her words coming out fast, something she does when she gets agitated. "You don't have to look a certain way, you know. You can just tell them all to fuck off."

I shrug my shoulders, look at the ground. Leah sits down next to me, defeated. After a few seconds of silence, she says, "Let's do something fun this weekend. Get your mind off this trash." She flips her long, dark hair off her shoulder.

"Oh ya, that reminds me," I say, rolling my eyes. "My mom made us hair appointments for back to school." But I didn't forget; I just knew Leah's reaction would be, well, less than excited.

Leah closes her eyes and falls dramatically back on my bed. "Why, why, why do you let her control you like this? And why do you always drag me along?"

"Because you're the only person who will pry my phone away from me. I need you to protect me from myself."

What's amazing about Leah is that she's a gentle artist but a fierce friend. And that's why I need her most. Because I've never been brave enough to tell anyone to fuck off, even if they really do deserve it, but Leah can never keep her mouth shut. And maybe she's dauntless because she has no shame to keep her down, or maybe the one secret she has does not exactly scare her.

An artist

My best friend Leah
who paints incongruous woman,
her brush strokes exploring wrongness:
beautiful women with monstrous hands
who can smother flames
women with arms long enough
to fully wrap around themselves
two or three times
women with eyes big like moons
which occupy more than half the face
restricting space for the nose and mouth
sometimes women
with claws instead of hands
or beaks instead of noses
or rubies instead of teeth
who rise out of the sea

Women who are grotesque
and also uncompromising

Leah who, despite her lack of interest,
has boys at our school lusting
who once, after overhearing a boy tell me at a party
that I was so lucky that Leah was my best friend
and did I ever see her naked?
told him every time she pictured *him* naked
she puked in her mouth
picturing his tiny balls and lack
of personality.

Leah
who has never confessed to anyone
except me
that she never pictures any boy naked
because she prefers the female body
(soft and delicate and round)
to any offered masculine frame.

4

A week later, at the hair salon, I am a hideous alien with pieces of foil clamped over sections of my hair. A large, green cape hugs my shoulders. Leah's beside me, spinning in her chair, playing music loudly on her phone until one of the old women tell her to turn it down. She sighs loudly.

A mother and her teenage daughter come in to have their hair done for a wedding. The daughter, I notice immediately, has Down syndrome and is noticeably giddy. Her mom brags to her hairdresser loudly so the whole salon will hear, "My beautiful daughter is going to a dance tonight," she swoons. "Do you want to see her dress? It's such a lovely color—the color of her eyes. Look--" she pulls out some pictures and women crowd around, smiling. "Doesn't she look amazing?" The ladies agree, nodding their heads. "My beautiful daughter," the mother croons.

Her daughter begs, "Mom, stop!" but smiles and plays along.

The mother cannot stop looking at her daughter. She is so proud. You would have thought her daughter had won the Nobel Peace Prize. But, her pride comes from the very simple fact that she loves her.

I do not think I've ever seen such a look of absolute and unadulterated love.

At first, the sight worries me—this poor girl, clearly different, could not possibly be seen,by anyone else, as this beautiful girl that her mother sees.

But then, I watch the pair with a fierce longing, wondering if my mother ever looked at me like this, and if she will forever hold me to an impossible standard.

"Hey, Star," Leah says, punching me lightly in the arm. "Are you crying *again*?"

I wipe at my eyes, silently cursing myself for being so goddamn emotional. "Nope," I say, "it must be the chemicals."

But Leah knows me too well. "He's not worth it," she says gently.

And I know Adam's not worth it, or at least I'm starting to realize it. That's not really the problem. It's that I can't stop thinking that I'm not worth anything. And so no wonder he couldn't possibly love me.

*   *   *   *

Leah and I drive to the beach for the last time before the fall air forges in and cools off the Atlantic. I have spent so many days hiding under dark covers in shaded rooms that Leah decides it's about time to confront the sunlight. Besides, school starts in a few days which means seeing Adam is inevitable.

Leah wears a bright, orange bikini that you could see even if standing a mile away. Her body, however, attracts more attention than her suit, but she, as always, remains oblivious to this as she runs, full sprint, into the ocean. I decide not to follow her in and instead sit on our blanket, hugging my knees.

I look at the inviting ocean water, wishing on the waves like I used to do when I was younger. I think of my mother with her strong arms and her long, thin legs and decide to keep my cover-up on over my bathing suit even though I love to swim and Leah ducks in and out of waves, calling my name over and over. My mother, who tells me how proud she is whenever I lose weight but does not understand what it takes: morning runs, afternoons at the gym, endless starvation and then inevitable binges followed by a desperate riddance of any overconsumption; and she will never understand how or why I always gain back every pound. My mother, who urged me to highlight my dark, leathery hair, who taught me to apply makeup to paint pretty over my flaws, who bought me all the latest trends, so that I would fit in (a seamless daughter), who loves me indefinitely but still encourages me to change everything.

I bury my toes in the sand and watch the little girl, who sits on a pink towel next to me, play. She wears a pink bathing suit with a white ruffle around the middle and a big, brimmed hat that looks too old for her age. It must be her mom's. Eventually, she brings two purple buckets down to the ocean and fills them up with water, and then runs back to her place in the sand, where she pours out the water, building mud castles and surrounding moats. She does this multiple times, until, once, on her walk back, the wind sweeps her hat off her head. She does not make any attempt to catch it--just watches it drift over a few feet and fall to the ground, right near the water. She looks at it quickly, but then decides her buckets are more important and races back to her castles, to fill her moat with water and mud.

I consider walking down to the water to retrieve her hat, but instead I close my eyes and feel a familiar sadness settle in. I think about sleeping but then feel drips of cold salt falling off Leah's nose and hair as she stands above me smiling, asking, "Why don't you love girls instead?"

"This coming from the girl who refuses to love anyone?" I say, taking off my sunglasses and reaching my hands up. Leah pulls me to standing, and we both shake off sand. Out of the corner of my eye, I see the little girl and her mother, walking away. They are in the distance now, trudging slowly through the sand, hand in hand.

"I'm not gonna put myself out there for just anyone," Leah says. "I'm waiting for someone who is good enough for my awesomeness. You need to work harder at loving yourself."

"You sound like a school guidance counselor but much more annoying," I say and walk over to the little girl's sand castle that now sits alone, abandoned. I consider stomping on it. Instead, I put back on my sunglasses and think about buying an oversized, obnoxious hat, realizing that I am definitely not ready for the light.

                    *   *   *   *

The night before I'm forced back to school, back to the place where Adam and I met, back to the hallways where he walked me to classes and pecked me on the cheek before we entered classrooms even though I hated how his dry lips tickled my cheek, I'm rifling through my closet trying to find the outfit that could help me fake being a knock-out, something that might make me look more like Mom. I've retried on all the clothes that she bought me, but every tight shirt only accentuates the wider parts of me that I want to disappear. I put on a long blue shirt that conceals my most hated parts and then quickly go into Mom's room to look in the able mirror.

While I'm practicing sucking in my gut, looking at my body from all angles in the tri-fold mirror, I can hear my mom right outside the door, humming softly. It's too late to make an escape so I pretend to look through her jewelry.

"Hey baby," she says, as she walks in the room. "You need anything for tomorrow?"

"Just some liposuction," I mutter under my breath.

"What, honey," she asks, distracted. She sits on the bed and kicks off her heels, starts taking off her earrings.

"Never mind Mom," I say motioning to her dresser. "Just looking for a necklace. Can I borrow one?"

She moves towards me and sifts through her basket of gold and silver. "Of course," she says. She picks up a necklace that's blue and sparkly. "How about this one?"

"It's pretty," I say, reaching for it. "Ya, thanks."

She smiles and opens her top drawer. "I'm exhausted," she yawns. "Thought I'd get in some comfortable clothes and relax with a movie. You interested?" She pulls out light purple, silk pajamas.

"I was just going to read, try to get my mind to turn off." I hold the necklace in my hands and try to avoid our reflections.

"Oh, Aster," she says, "you just wait. When I'm done remaking you, all the boys will be drooling." She sits down on her bed and starts to fold her pajamas even though she'll put them on soon.

There it is again: that promise my mother has made since I was a little girl. I remember when I had my first "boyfriend" in first grade, this kid named Lance. For a week straight, he brought me little gifts--a balloon, candy, mechanical pencils. It was a great romance until I missed school one day because I was sick and Lance couldn't wait for me so he gave my gift to another girl. I was devastated but Mom pulled me close, told me boys would be chasing me some day. I just continue to wonder when this day will come and hate that it's something I want more than anything else.

"Ok mom thanks. But really it's my junior year so I need to start focusing on my work if I'm going to go to college for writing. My guidance counselor says I need to work on my portfolio. Maybe it's good that things didn't work out with Adam so I can focus more on writing. "

Mom looks disappointed. She finishes folding and puts her hands in her lap. "Of course writing is important to you," she says. "But you've always done well in school. Have you thought more about what we talked about? Maybe looking into business school? There's really not much money in the arts."

"Do you think I should give up on writing?" I cross my arms, agitated. I know I don't want the answer, so why do I ask?

"No," she says quickly. "I mean, never. It's just that I want you to be happy…"

"I am happy," I say softly. "I'm fine. I want to be a writer."

"Okay, I'm just asking you to look at all of your options." Mom stands up and goes to the mirror to brush her hair. She can never sit still. "Hey, I was thinking," she says to me, speaking to my reflection in her mirror. "Do you want to sign up for this new weight loss APP? I forget what it's called, but I have a girlfriend at work who just lost thirty pounds from using it. We could do it together. It will be fun." She turns around to look at me.

I stare at her bony arms and slim waist. "But you don't need to lose any weight," I say.

"Well, I know, but it will keep me on track so I don't gain any." She smiles. "You know your grandad used to call me fatty. When I was younger than you even, he would poke me in the belly and tell me to stop eating so much ice cream."

My little Italian grandfather, from what I remember,

was constantly smiling, always trying to get Luke and me to play corny games with him. He'd steal our noses and perform a magic trick where it looked like he could separate his thumb. All I ever saw him drink was beer, and he even let us have little sips when our parents weren't looking, but the thought of him even thinking mean thoughts surprises me. "That's awful," I say. "I didn't know Gramps was ever mean."

"Well, he thought he was being funny, but I never laughed," Mom answers as she folds and refolds silk. "I got made fun of in school sometimes too. I was always fat, and I hated it."

"Mom, you were never fat!" I say, incredulous. I think back to Mom's old pictures from her childhood and high school. She didn't keep many, and she never wanted anyone to see them. From the ones I had seen, I had never thought "fat." I *had* thought, *wow, she looked just like me.* Compared to her small size now, I guess she was almost twice the size. Am I twice her size?

"Aster, you're sweet," she rolls her eyes. "Anyways, later I grew up and realized I could change my body. And so I did. And after that I realized I could change anything about my life. So I did. You know, I grew up poor. We didn't have much. No one even mentioned college to me. Well, you know the rest." She uses one hand to pretend to write, narrating the remaining parts of her story in the air.

And of course I know this story already; it is one that I loved hearing over and over when I was young. A fairy tale with my mom as the princess who saves herself. My mom graduated from high school with no real prospects. A few years later, she married my dad (who she had met through a friend.) He wanted to have children immediately, and she acquiesced since that was what most women her age were doing and had Luke. But, she did not feel at all fulfilled. Instead, she felt empty, and she didn't want to be poor anymore. My Dad was still not yet making good money as an apprentice so, while a neighbor watched Luke, she worked all day at a local bank and saved up money on her own to go to school at night. Eventually, one of her college professors fell madly in love with her even though he was married ("nothing happened, ever" mom claimed) and did everything in his power to get her a job with a stand-out company in the city. My mom, with her strengths and independence, conquered every job she had and became her own boss. She often tied her success to her beauty, and I didn't want this to be the case. Regardless, she achieved anything she vowed to do. So, when Luke was five, she felt so powerful, able to come from nothing and then buy a large home in a rich neighborhood, and she wanted to pass on not only her success, but also what she believed was enchanted beauty to her boy but also a daughter to whom she could impart her secrets. So, of course, because my mom can make magic happen, I was born.

"And you can have it all too," Mom continues. "You know Luke; he just settles. But you don't. You're just like me."

"I guess," I mumble, conflicted. Part of me wants to be just like her--to have her beauty and confidence, her power for business, her dreams of money, but the other part of me likes the quiet, the uncomplicated, the plain.

"Have you talked to your brother lately?" Mom changes the subject and stands up, gathers her silk, putting an end to the conversation. I want to curl up with her like I did when I was young, ask her to read me a story that might actually come true. Or ask her if maybe she could just accept that this is the only me there will ever be.

"Is that a joke?" I ask instead. "Luke's like a complete stranger now. Well, he always felt like a stranger, honestly."

"I know," Mom sighs, sad resolve written on her face. "He always just did his own thing. That's why I'm so lucky to have you." She takes the necklace I'm still holding in my hands and slips it around my neck. "You're my incarnate, so I'll always be young." She laughs at her little joke, but I don't think it's funny. "I'll look into that weight loss APP tomorrow and see about signing us up," she says.

"Okay," I say. As I watch her leave, my hand

clasps the necklace that feels warm from her touch, and I wonder if, in my own fairy tale, she's the villain.

*   *   *   *

I wander down to Luke's empty room and sit on his twin bed. My parents keep his room the way it's been for years, all dark colors and black and white art on the walls. Even some of his old clothes hang in the closet. There's a clock on the small, bedside table and an old baseball glove.

I used to love listening to my dad and Luke play catch. I never liked to play it myself; whenever Dad threw me the ball, it stung my hand and Luke was too gentle, throwing the ball underhand. I couldn't find a happy medium.

So instead, I'd lie on the grass between their pass and close my eyes, imagining the onomatopoeia of their game. I'd muse how the ball made a *slap* sound, but that was too vague. It was lighter than that, and friendlier, like a *squish* but more of a subtle suction sound that I had trouble naming. The ball releases from Luke's hand, silence besides the hum of the air outside and the rustle of leaves if it was fall, as the ball moves up and up…Dad's glove rises and then *thwunk.*

As Luke grew older, he became more of a loner, preferring to play by himself than with friends or even Dad. He also was afflicted with really bad migraines which, by the time he turned fifteen, were so bad that he'd have to give himself a shot when he felt a headache coming on. Dad painted his bedroom walls a dark purple, almost black, and installed darkening shades to his windows after Luke explained that darkness helped mitigate the pain. If he wasn't sleeping off a migraine in his dark room, he still shut himself in there to draw comics. He was, and probably still is, obsessed with superheroes and he could draw them pretty well too, the ones that he would let me see.

When he was sixteen and my parents gave him his first car, we barely saw him. He worked landscaping during the warmer months and plowed during the winters. He had a few friends, I think, but we never really met any of them. Whenever he was home, he locked himself in his room and turned his speaker volume up high, listening to older music like James Taylor. Stuff that no one else in the house liked. He was so much older, but I still felt stranded when he didn't come down for dinner or he completely ignored Dad's request to have a pass. As I grew older, I became more aware of the distance between Luke and my parents, and I didn't understand how he could be so cold to two people who genuinely loved him. My parents weren't perfect but they were always loving and generous with both of us. Sometimes, I relished in the fact that I got all of the attention; other times, I hated Luke for leaving me to fulfill all their grand expectations, especially Mom's.

But mostly I felt sad that I lived right next door to this hostage who looked just like me—same green eyes and thick and wavy, brown hair. I wanted so badly to make a connection with him, we all did, but we didn't speak the same language. I relished in words and sounds, the *crinkle* of a turned page, the *whir* of Dads drill, but Luke drowned us all out by putting on headphones and forgetting to answer our calls. On the surface, he was a good kid; he never yelled back, never rebelled, always did his chores, got good grades. He just exercised indifference to just about everything that mattered to our little family.

His egress from all of our lives was so slow that we did not have time to mourn the loss of him, and I learned the sounds of his life, the only pieces of him that remained loud enough to hear. The quiet *click* of closed doors. The *squeak* from underneath his footsteps as he tiptoed down the hall. The *roar* of his engine when he was heading to *Oregon State,* his left hand clumsily waving through the window as we stood on the front lawn feeling some sense of relief that we could finally say good-bye.

Tethered

I was the golden child
I was the compliant anchor
so that our parents
did not hear the hush
of your absence

And so I tethered
my own good behavior
to their rocky surf
performed cheap smiles and graceful tricks
to prevent their sail
from drifting in strong winds

So when Dad needed help
he called out to you first
but your boat had become
an almost invisible fragment
in the deep waters
I'd throw him life rafts
rescue him
from the icy chill of abandoned ships

And if Mom wanted me to be pretty
I'd let her braid my metal links
and dress me in frills
let her
securely fasten my chains
to her glistening fantasy
of an ocean song

{ FALL }

5

Leah picks me up on the first morning of school, a hot and hazy day already. I wear dark yoga pants with an oversized black and scarlet top.

"Are you in mourning?" Leah asks, as I lean into the seat.

"Leave my funk alone," I say and turn up the music: Adele of course, the sound of heartbreak.

"Are you ready?"Leah asks, more compassionately, and I know she's asking, not about the upcoming school year, but about how I will have to confront Adam for the first time since I found out he cheated, and also the girl who stole his heart.

"Let's just hope that they're not in any of my

classes," I say.

"Are you okay? Are you, like, still in love with him?" Leah asks.

I stare hard at the road in front of me. "You know what? To be honest, I don't know. I definitely don't want to get back together. It's just that, I don't know, I'm *embarrassed.* Like, everyone knows and I can't stop wondering what's wrong with me? And does everyone else wonder what's wrong with me?"

"Nothing is *wrong* with *you,*" Leah shouts (since she's repeated this maybe a thousand times these last few weeks). "*He's* just an *asshole.* Case closed. No detective work needed. Now pull over so I can remind you what a fucking smile looks like."

"No, no. I got it. Okay, okay. Happy is on," I say, touching my bottom and top teeth together, and pulling my lips apart into a semblance of a smile.

"Good. Now, onto more important first-day-of-school business, yes? Like, do you think Sarah finally bleached her mustache? And, will Mr. Bishop actually sleep with one of his students this year? And I'm just *dying* to know if Jules is actually going to admit that she did make out with an eighth grader over the summer. I mean, we already know it's true--why the hell is she trying to hide it."

"This coming from the girl who--" I begin, but Leah cuts me off.

"Shut it, Star."

*   *   *   *

Everyone at my school knows Adam Hollow, or at least they know his family, because the Hollows are undeniably the wealthiest family in our small town. Adam's mom owns an elegant bridal boutique and his dad is a corporate lawyer.

I only knew Adam from a distance like most people at our school even though we were in some of the same classes; he had transferred from an all boys private school at the beginning of my sophomore year (rumor was that he got kicked out for making joints out of the pages he ripped from a Bible). To me, he seemed more like a character than a real person so when he came up to me last year and asked me to the homecoming dance, I struggled to string some words together but apparently managed to say yes. When the richest boy in school asks you out, there's only one answer, especially since Adam has a commanding nature that encourages people to just go along with what he asks.

I didn't know much about him, but I felt like the luckiest girl in school. My heart hummed the week before the dance as I recalled stories from my childhood. I had lived a normal, somewhat monotonous life so far and here was my opportunity. Here is when my life would change, and maybe, just maybe, I could be seen as beautiful; finally, the powers my mom stored for me would be unearthed.

Adam wasn't exactly popular or well-liked, but he had his own small group of friends who joined us in the limo to take us to the dance. We were the only students riding in style that night and I would have been embarrassed (how unnecessary to take a limo to a dance that's not prom) but I was so caught up in my fairy tale moment that I didn't care.

I wore a light blue dress that my mom, who was more than eager after hearing about who had asked me, helped me pick out. Adam looked older than necessary in a suit jacket and tight, military haircut. Sort of like an aged high school football coach at the end of the season banquet. Was he cute? Sort of. But he was certainly assertive and unhesitating, and I wanted to fit, neat and snug, into my own fairy tale.

All night, he made me laugh, mainly by mocking the jocks that were dancing aggressively with their dates, and, towards the end of the night, he swept me across the dance floor. "You know why I asked you to this dance?" he asked, staring at me so intently with creamy, brown eyes that I felt woozy.

"I have no idea," I said dreamily, wondering if my glass slippers were touching the ground.

"Because my mom knows your mom and said you needed a date," he whispered into my ear. "She must need your mom's business or something. She said if I asked you then I could end my groundation early."

"Oh," I said, looking away, my shoes now lead on the floor. Not slippers at all, just cheap flats from Payless. "I'm sorry, I never said-"

I put my palms on his chest to push him away, but he tightened his arms around my waist. "No, don't be sorry. I'm glad I asked. I like you. I didn't expect to."

I hooked my hands back around his neck. "Thanks?" I said slowly.

At the end of the night, he kissed me. It was not particularly romantic since I still couldn't figure out if he actually liked me or not, but it was better that my first kiss with Tommy Pecina, in eighth grade, at a high school football game where a group of our friends circled around us and dared us to lock lips for five seconds...one...two...three...I had put my hand in the air and counted with my fingers...four...five...until he took his mouth away from mine.

Adam and I kissed but I didn't count the seconds; it lasted for one song, and then a chaperone tapped him on the shoulder.

So it wasn't Cinderella's ball but I still stupidly felt that he could be my happily ever after.

*   *   *   *

Adam did not want to follow in his parent's footsteps; he wanted to be a drummer, something his dad tried his damndest to prevent by enrolling him in every academic extracurricular possible. His parents expected him to get straight A's in school, go to an Ivy League college, and study business or law. Adam overslept most days, smoked pot, and believed college was for phonies.

We spent a lot of time in Adam's car. He would get high then pick me up, drive me through town. He was smart and I'm not sure anyone else listened to him--not his parents, definitely not his pothead friends. He would give me tours of the rich neighborhoods, spewing history and facts about our town and the old rich for what seemed like hours. He'd talk about his love for drumming, his future as a musician, his favorite bands, his love for Stephen Perkins and Keith Moon. He'd talk about his parents, how hard he worked to *not* be like them, how they didn't understand him. He talked about everything from solar systems to deep sea fishing. His voice never paused, and I liked the way it sounded: a low baritone with an immature accent on certain word endings, like when he added a -w to an -er sound where it didn't belong, so, if you listened closely, it sounded more like computew, paper more like papew; it made him sound childish which softened his arrogant exterior.

He didn't leave much room for my responses; he seemed to end every sentence with a definitive period. No ellipsis so that I could finish his thought. No question mark so that I could answer. No exclamation point even so that I could give back an equally emotional response. I mean, sometimes he'd ask me if I agreed with something he said, which I often did (I guess) but mostly I'd sit in the passenger seat and nod along. Sometimes I'd yawn, settle back in my seat and close my eyes. I'd daydream. I imagined that maybe he looked over, at some point, to make sure I was still listening, but now I'm not entirely sure. Those car rides felt like long lectures with no real pattern or thread. It's a wonder I kept getting back into his car. It's just that I felt so lucky, still. That I was his girl. That he picked me (even if not by choice, at first.)

But really, what did I feel? What was that feeling that I should have named? Because so many times, I felt heaviness in my chest, I felt too much air in my throat. While Adam said thousands of words during those car rides, I became...I felt....empty. Adam noticed too. I remember, one night, only weeks before we broke up, he asked me why I was so quiet all of the time.

"Hmmm?" I murmured, "I'm not quiet."

"Yes, you are. You're always quiet. You never say anything." He sounded mad.

"I'm just...listening." We were holding hands. I squeezed.

"Okay." He squeezed back. "But sometimes it's boring. Being with you."

We ended up at Shay Park, a little pond with mountain peaks and starry nights and he kissed me in the back seat until my lips numbed. At some point, I told Adam I needed some air and when I got out of the car, I leaned against it feeling weak. I was offended by what Adam had said about me being boring, but the most hurtful part was that I wasn't quiet at all. If he knew me, like Leah did or my father did or even my mother, he would know that I loved to talk, I loved words, I loved writing poetry.

I had missed my words when I was with Adam, but I didn't know what I would say without him.

*   *   *   *

I walk into Austen High, a large, old building seemingly right in the center of mountains and head straight for class to avoid the hallways where I can feel Adam's presence. My goals today are simple: lay low, ignore Adam, survive.

On top of my fear of seeing him, I am also anxious about my first class called "The Power of Words." My guidance counselor who, thanks to my dad, knows I love to write, encouraged me to take it. Even though I have written in journals since kindergarten, and I always dreamt I'd be a writer someday, I've only ever written for myself.

A friend had told me that the teacher, Mrs. Skye, is a "hard-core feminist" who has too high expectations of her students, but when I walk into room 212 and look around, I feel somewhat at ease. Posters of famous writers, mostly women, hang on all four corners of the room. I read some of the names underneath: Sylvia Plath, Alice Walker, Louise Erdrich. There are books *everywhere--*

stacked neatly on bookshelves, counters, and tables. I want to live here.

The classroom is arranged in a large circle so that we can all see each other. I sit in a desk by a window and look around at unfamiliar faces and see there are only girls, most of whom I don't really know because they are either Artsy or Theater, two groups Leah and I typically avoid due to their dyed pink and purple hair and boyish, unmatched clothes. But not knowing a single soul does nothing to quell my anxiety; strangers or friends, I don't know that I'm ready to share my own words.

The girl next to me has shoulder length hair dyed platinum blond with streaks of pink. I have never seen her before. She wears black from head to toe and even has painted black nails. Yet, all of her dark attire cannot mask her soft, feminine features.

"Do you have an extra pen?" she asks me, her voice soft and dreamy like white sand. "I can't believe I forgot a pen on the first day of school."

"Of course," I say and hand her one of mine.

"Thanks. You're Aster, right?" she asks.

"Yea," I say, a little surprised because the girl doesn't look at all familiar to me. "I'm sorry, I don't remember meeting you…"

"Oh, I'm Mollie. My sister, Beth, runs track with

you. Or used to." She takes the pen and doodles on her notebook.

I know Beth well. We were on the same 4 by 1 relay team. "Oh ya," I say, watching her draw tiny birds on her page. "I quit going into my sophomore year."

"How come?"

Before I can respond, Mrs. Skye walks briskly into the room at the exact same time the bell rings. She is a substantially large woman with long, thin hair, and a perfectly round face. She sits down in an open student desk in the circle with us, one solitary book on her desk, and adjusts her circular glasses. I can hear her breathing from across the room, a labored sound.

"Sorry I'm late or, I guess, just on time." She looks at the clock. "I really had every intention of getting here before you. Well, good morning class," she says, smiling as she looks around the room. "I see, as usual, that the men in this school are still uncomfortable with women's voices." I smile and some of the girls laugh softly. "Or the rumor is still going around that I'm a feminist and hate men," she laughs. "Well, let's introduce ourselves and then we'll discuss the course expectations."

For introductions, she asks us to find a poem or lyric or passage that we love and share it with the class as well as explain what thrills us when it comes to these words. "I want to know what, exactly, about the words make you temporarily stop breathing," she says and then gives us some time to look up what we want to share on our phones or notebooks. I know the poem I will share, so, unsure of what to do, I pull out a book and flip through the pages. My heart pounds loudly; I have never enjoyed speaking in front of a class. Why couldn't my first class of the day be easy? Why couldn't I just sit here quietly, pretend to listen to the boring explanation of the course, and sink deeper into another miserable school year?

When the class is ready, Mrs. Skye asks us to stand up, share our names and the piece of writing, along with our explanation. "Who wants to begin?"

It's no surprise that Naomi, star of every school play since elementary school, raises her hand eagerly. "I'm Naomi," she says loudly, smiling and looking around the circle. "One of my favorite lines is said by Emily Webb who I played in *Our Town* last year. She says, 'do human beings ever realize life while they live it?--every, every minute?' This line spoke to me because I *do* live every moment to the fullest…"

As Naomi drones on about her fantastic, ideal life, Mollie looks over at me and rolls her eyes. I smile. Naomi's optimism isn't poisoning just me I guess.

The other girls share rather general, well-known writings, similar to Naomi. Piper, a senior, quotes

Juliet. Rachel, who actually has a see through shirt on, shares a poem by ee cummings. Isabelle, a girl I recognize from one of Leah's art classes, quotes Andy Warhol. Mrs. Skye nods enthusiastically at each girl and then asks follow-up questions about their choices; their conversations seem effortless, but my heart still pounds in my ears as I try to calm my nerves.

When it's my turn, I stand up and feel my face get hot. "My name is Aster and I'm a junior. I love every poem by Sarah Kay, but this is the beginning of one of my favorites." I read with a shaky voice: "If I should have a daughter, instead of 'Mom,' she's going to call me 'Point B,' because that way she knows that no matter what happens, at least she can always find her way to me. And I'm going to paint solar systems on the backs of her hands so she has to learn the entire universe before she can say, 'Oh, I know that like the back of my hand.' And she's going to learn that this life will hit you hard in the face, wait for you to get back up just so it can kick you in the stomach. But getting the wind knocked out of you is the only way to remind your lungs how much they taste of air. There is hurt, here, that cannot be fixed by Band-Aids or poetry."

I pause, willing my hands to stop trembling and wait for Mrs. Skye to respond. "Beautiful," she says, "why do you love this?"

"It just says so much about fear, and about how parents cannot always protect their children from pain. I don't know. This is what every child wants, I think. To know that there will be someone always waiting for you on the other side of the pain."

"Well said," Mrs. Skye says. "And I agree. I hope that everyone in this room has a point B. Do you?"

Do I? The question rattles me.

"Oh, sorry, I always ask too many probing questions!" Mrs. Skye says, saving me from answering her question.

There's silence until, finally, the girl next to me stands, "My name is Mollie and I'm a freshman and I think it's only fitting that I share a lyric from my favorite song." And then she starts to speak quietly and seriously. At first, I wince, embarrassed for this young girl who does not yet understand some of the social rules of high school. But then, as she approaches the chorus, she brings her closed hand up to her mouth and sings into an invisible microphone, and I realize she is, quite comically, reciting Miley Cyrus's "I Can't Be Tamed": "I can't be tamed/I can't be blamed/I can't be, can't, I can't be tamed."

Mollie's performance has everyone laughing, even Mrs. Skye who begins to clap along. At the end of the lyric, Mollie bows. "I feel like the reason I love these words is self-explanatory. I can't be tamed. Not by anyone. Miley nailed it."

"This is your theme song then," Mrs. Skye says, "I think wildness is best."

After Mrs. Skye quickly goes over the course expectations (the most boring part of my job besides lunch duty, she explains), she gives us our first assignment. "I feel really inspired by the words you all shared during introductions today. I want you to borrow or allude to them--maybe a word, maybe a phrase. And I want you to write a poem where you incorporate these power words. Your poem can revolve around the words or you can merely mention them in a line. We will share these with the class tomorrow before digging into rhetoric."

Mollie and I gather our things and smile shyly at each other. "I can't wait to hear how you incorporate 'I can't be tamed' into a poem."

"It's going to be epic," Mollie says, "and when I'm done I'm gonna tape it to my ex boyfriends locker." And even though she's two years younger, I can't resist feeling inspired.

*   *   *   *

When I walk into my French III class, the teacher, Madame Sharpel, tells us, since it's our third year of French, that we will no longer speak in English. She tells us to find a small group and talk to each other in French about our summer. Two girls sitting next to me, Sara and Mariah, slide their desks over and speak nonsense. I have never been good at second languages and can barely say menial phrases, so I nod, pretend to follow along, end up doodling poetry instead, tinkering with words and sounds on my notebook's page while pretending to listen.

Eventually, I'm distracted by the boy in front of me who looks a little familiar. He's conversing with the teacher like he's a native speaker. He's sort of cute but his t-shirt, with a big picture of the old rapper Biggie, looks funny on him.

"Avez-vous voyagé partout cet été?" he asks her. He is overly friendly with teeth too big for his mouth and height too tall for the desks.

Madame Sharpel, clearly impressed, uses the next few minutes of class to berate the rest of us for not being able to hold a conversation in our second language. The class groans, but the boy just grins, explaining his adoration "pour une telle belle langue." He is not the least bit ashamed of his role as teacher's pet.

"Quel est votre nom?" she asks him.

"Mon nom est Levi," he says with a shiny voice and, while I try to stop it, his name gets stuck in my pen so that the ink leaks the letters onto my paper.

My day is going so well

That I actually forget about...
everything

And I have this feeling
that I can't name
it feels...different

What is it?
Not happiness,
but hope maybe?

Not clarity,
but resolve?

Whatever it is,
it begins to dissolve,
when I walk into the cafeteria
and am confronted by Adam Hollow

Just because Adam cheated on me,

And has a new girlfriend already,
who is, right now, sitting
so closely (like centimeters)
next to him at the lunch table,
the table where I used to sit,
doesn't mean
I don't exist anymore.

So why do I feel so *infinitesimal?*
When he puts his arm around her
and moves his plate of fries
to share.

I desperately try to act *imperturbable*
but my goddamn peripheral vision
won't lose the sight
of their skin touching

words are armor
I eat them instead
of my sandwich

words are solace
I write them down on a napkin
before wiping my mouth

> I am *viable*
> He is *spume*
> She is *pustule*

I look up, away from their table

but they walk by me,
holding hands,
only a foot away
Liz is *ethereal*--
she actually waves at me
like she's a queen

Proving, once and for all,
that my feelings are *picayune*
and in this *polyphonic* cafeteria
a *cataclysm* shatters
my foolish hope.

6

That night, I do all of my homework for other classes before approaching my first writing assignment for Mrs. Skye. I've been thinking about Point B all day but am unable to nail it down with words. I know the poem is about having a person you can depend on, believing in the support they give you to pull you through any struggle. But when I think of Point B, it's what I want most in life, and, when finally there, I will find happiness. It's not a person who lifts me up; instead, a body that I can live in and love.

When Mom knocks on my door an hour later, I still haven't written much. I'm just staring at a blank computer screen.

"How was your first day?" she asks and sits on my bed.

"Fine. I think I'm really going to like one of my elective courses," I start, "it's all about the power of words and my teacher is absolutely brilliant and…"

I trail off as mom smiles mildly, her eyes glazing over. She's a CEO of a company, not a writer. Her passion is money, not words.

"So did you see Adam? Did he comment on your new look?" she asks hopefully.

There's that punch in the stomach again.

"No I didn't see him today," I lie. "I think it's better that I keep my distance. And I don't think he'd really notice that I look different. He's sort of fully focused on another girl at the moment."

"Well, make him notice you! You could be so beautiful if you--"

"Mom, please!" I interrupt her before she reminds me, yet again, of my shortcomings. "I really have work to do." I motion to my computer, exasperation creeping into my voice.

"Sure, sorry. I just want you to have a good year, that's all."

I turn back to my computer screen, ignoring her as best I can, tears forming in my eyes, until she gets the hint and leaves.

I look at the pictures I've taped to my mirror: my point B. If only I could figure out how to get there from here.

*   *   *   *

"Good morning, girls. I thought we would start our class today by sharing the poems we wrote for homework. As I mentioned yesterday, you are going to be doing a lot of writing and a lot of sharing so we might as well get used to it." Mrs. Skye folds her hands on her desk and smiles. "Who would like to start?"

My printed poem is on my desk; my palms are already sweating. I read it over quickly as Mrs. Skye waits for someone to volunteer, and I think *there's no way I'm passing this in*. Why didn't I write something less personal?

When I look up, I see the girls around me must be feeling the same way. Everyone looks down or out the window. Mrs. Skye lets the seconds tick by. "Okay," she says after a few minutes. "Looks like we have a lot of work to do when it comes to sharing our writing. Let's start small today. Why don't you all find a partner and swap your work. I want you all to comment on each other's work and then I will give you tonight to revise."

I let out a long, relieved breath. Mollie, dressed again in all black, asks if I'd like to work with her.

"Yes, please," I say, discreetly hiding my poem in my notebook. "I actually didn't do the assignment," I lie.

"That's okay. I won't tell. We'll just work on mine."

Point B
By Aster Lamonte

Every year it seems
usually in health class
we watch a movie where a young girl
suffers from an eating disorder

Usually it's about a gymnast
where she undergoes therapy
and "overcomes" her struggles.

This year, we discuss a movie
but mostly anorexia and bulimia
with our teacher, Mrs. Johnson,
who looks bitter and tired
even after her long vacation away from us

We sleep with eyes open
as she lectures us about the dangers
of eating disorders.

And I know this talk
aims to scare me
or make me aware
of succumbing to such a disease
but instead,
I dream about the possibility
of thinness
and think,
just like every other year,
I wish I could have that much self-control
to starve myself.

7

Leah and I only have one class together, and of course it's with the most sexist gym teacher, Mr. Sergi. He doesn't even glance up from his newspaper when we walk into the gym, but Max, star quarterback gets a handshake and a congratulations for leading the team to victory on game 1. Max is wearing a "Make America Great Again" hat even though hats aren't allowed in the school building. He smiles, a real golden boy.

"Proud of you boy," Mr. Sergi says and Leah pretend gags before sitting on the gym floor, crossing her legs, criss-cross-apple-sauce, like we did in kindergarten.

Rumor is that Mr. Sergi divides the girls and boys to play different games so the ladies "don't break a nail." He is well-known for calling the boys "little women" or "Marys" if they get hurt and if a girl gets aggressive he tells her to "act more like a lady." I always lacked faith in the validity of these stories--what are we living in the 1950's?--until he had run into me and Leah in the hallway one day last year after school and asked us to go find some boys to help him lift some equipment. When we both offered to help him, he actually laughed out loud and then repeated his request for "real men."

The only positive to having a sexist teacher who is entirely uncomfortable with the language of females is that, rumor has it, girls can get away with pretty much anything. Most of the girls in our school who have had him as a teacher learned pretty fast that they could sit out on any day if they mention their "time of the month."

When Mr. Sergi finally addresses the entire class, I can't help thinking that you can measure a middle aged man's happiness based on the size of his beer belly and the condition of his sneakers. And, after assessing his giant, pregnated belly and old, scuffed shoes warped from his extra weight, it's safe to say he spends most nights alone, eating chicken wings on a fold up dinner table and wiping his mouth with his sleeve. Mr. Sergi drones on and on about proper rules, healthy expectations (ironic, right?), and his love for "the game." Which game? We weren't intent to find out.

Next to me, Leah's trying her best to keep her eyes open. I elbow her and she pulls out her phone, starts scrolling through her Instagram.

Across from us, Max keeps looking at Leah, but it's not the look I'm used to seeing, the look of complete adoration. Instead, his top lip curls in disapproval.

I nudge her again and then point in his direction

when he's not looking. "What?" she whispers.

I nod in Max's direction. "Do you know him?"

She shrugs. "Not really. Just that he's a football player. He's cute I guess. Oh, and he wants to make America great again." She shoots him a quick middle finger but he doesn't see.

But, moments later, his eyes are back on her and the way he narrows his eyes unnerves me. But Leah's brazen as usual. "Yo," she calls. He nods at her and she responds slowly, announcing each word: "What...the fuck...are you...looking at?"

He opens his mouth to answer but Sergi's loud voice stops him, "Hey, no swearing! Didn't anyone ever teach you to act like a--"

"Don't you dare say Lady," Leah interrupts.

Sergi's face turns red from rage. "Young La-"

"I'm not a fucking lady," Leah says, calm as hell.

"Office. Now," Sergi sputters, and points towards the door dramatically.

Leah collects her stuff and I watch silently. Max eyes her coldly. When Leah leaves the room, his eyes follow her. Then, he asks Coach if he can go get some water. "Sure," Sergi says, "quickly. We need you in the game." As if gym class actually counts for something. Max leaves and there's no way he's thirsty.

"Mr. Sergi, can I go too?" I ask.

"Absolutely not," he bellows. "Sit!"

I'm never worried about Leah; she can take on anyone. But the way Max pulled his hat down low, barely covering an arrogant smirk, before following Leah out the gym doors, leaves me with the same dread I felt years ago when mean kids excluded her because of her dark skin, before they all wanted to sleep with her or be like her. "Um Mr. Sergi? I have to go to the nurse. I think I just got my--"

He puts his hand up to stop the blasphemous word. "Just go!"

*   *   *   *

I run quickly through the gym doors and down the hallway towards the main office. When I get there, I see Leah sitting in one of the office chairs, looking bored. She laughs when she sees me. "What are you doing?"

"Max followed you out," I say, breathless. "Did he say anything to you?"

"Haven't seen him," she says, unconcerned by my nerves, my fast-beating heart. "Just waiting for the principal to finish up a meeting. I'm sure he'll want to set me straight." She smirks. "*You* okay?"

"Fine, just be careful," I warn. "Max seems messed up."

"Thanks, Mom," Leah teases.

No one's sitting at the front desk so I go back out into the hallway and walk around nervously, but Max is nowhere to be found. When I walk back in, Leah's gone, probably in the principal's office by now. I walk back to the gym and there's Max, playing lacrosse, yelling plays at everyone, as if they care.

Mr. Sergi tells me I can sit out for the rest of class. Relieved, I sit on the bleachers, watching. When the bell rings, I hurry towards the locker room and almost run into Max but he barely glances at me. In this moment, I actually feel glad that, in this school, I'm mostly invisible.

*　　　*　　　*　　　*

On weekends, at Leah's house no one bothers us, since her mom, dressed in high, black boots and tight shirts that embellish her small waist and round breasts, kisses us both on the cheek around dinner time on Friday and then disappears and will not reemerge until the week begins.

Leah's dad left before first grade and she rarely mentions him, except for those rare times when she pulls out her family album, flipping through pictures slowly, agonizing over this lost ghost who hovers above them, even though she and her mom are always present and smiling.

Leah's mom is different now, not happy exactly, but not sad either; instead, a little reckless but mostly alive, willing to meet men in dark places and exchange mouths and secrets. When we were younger, Leah and I used to stretch our bodies beneath a mirror that hung on Candace's ceiling and giggle while we put our limbs in pretzel positions before we realized the purpose of such a mirror and then, just like with her father, we never mentioned its existence.

Tonight, Leah insists we go to a party at Melody's house, Leah's friend, who she met at work this summer. Even though Melody is a year younger, apparently her house is the place to be since her mom works overnight shifts and her dad is another lost ghost.

Leah and I can't share clothes because we aren't nearly the same size but luckily we can share makeup, shoes, jewelry. I don't usually wear makeup but Leah insists on giving me "smokey eyes." I don't even want to show my face at a party, let alone dress up for one. And I know Leah's just trying to help but it's hard to accept that her simple jeans and black t-shirt that she threw on a minute ago looks better than every attempt I've made at looking presentable.

Sometimes I think the jealousy I harbor in my heart and my thoughts will eventually eat me alive. I wish my mom was right and that running could somehow help me solve, or at least escape, my conflicted feelings. I'd burn my jealousy off like calories, sweat it out of these monstrous, green eyes. I hate this feeling, especially when the person on the other end of it is my best friend who loves me and means no harm.

"Close your eyes," she pouts at me, eye shadow brush in hand. "Not so hard," she says when I clamp them shut.

"Make up your mind," I say.

She sighs through her mouth and I can feel her hot breath on my face. She holds my chin with her hand and smoothes color on my eyelids.

I imagine that I'm her palette and, because of those colors, like her paintings, a more beautiful picture will appear, even though the result might be mismatched. In the end, her paintings always take my breath away.

Or maybe I'll look more like her if I wish for it hard enough.

Eventually, she tells me to go look in the mirror. "You know, my mirror you can actually see your reflection in," she teases. "Open your eyes," she says and I can hear the clicks of her compacts shutting.

I resist and keep my eyes closed for a moment, imagining that when I open them, I really will look different. But as always, the mirror reflects the same face; I smile but it just makes my nose look bigger. I tilt my head to the side and warn myself silently, as always, that this is my eternity. I sing in my head, *I'm a little teapot, short and stout.*

"Sexy," Leah declares. I know she says it to make me feel better, but I just roll my eyes. Teapots can never be sexy.

*   *   *   *

Melody's house is the size of a small shed and young bodies surround the run-down outside like moths. Who would know there is a beautiful goddess inside?

Although I've only met her once, Melody still pulls me in for a long hug that feels genuine despite the booze on her breath.

"I'm so happy you came!" she squeals and hooks her arm through mine, quickly sweeping me through the house and into the kitchen.

There's not one clear spot: every room is littered with beer cans, food, cups. I don't know anyone here, so I awkwardly stand against the wall. Eventually, every male moth is attracted to the light and makes a circle around Leah offering her drinks, telling jokes to hear her laugh, pretending they can't stand straight in order to lean into her.

Melody rolls her eyes and takes my hand, "We should take a shot," she yells over the music. I'm disoriented from the noise and my own nervousness but I automatically count the calories in my head because I promised Mom I'd join that stupid program with her. I already had a beer so maybe 150 but I barely ate lunch and a straight shot with no mix might be less.

What the hell? I think and follow her outside, slightly mesmerized by her graceful walk, hips swaying side to side, long mermaid hair cascading behind.

There it is again: Point B. It's like I can never escape it.

We take shots of the cheapest liquor and wash it down with beer. I'm feeling buzzed and almost happy, forget all about counting, but then Melody gets swept into the tide of rolling music and laughter and, feeling suddenly alone, I'm left to float, sidestepping the pulsing bodies.

And I almost leave, but then I see Levi.

No one ever remembers my name.
at school
or at parties, I introduce myself
and my name, forgotten,
by the time he drinks his beer
and finds the courage to approach Leah
or someone with a similar, silvery body

I am never enough
to be remembered.

So, I stand in corners
with a sneer
on my face
conjuring up frozen images
so that I appear
cold as ice pretending
I don't want warm conversation

I envision
a sharp icicle ready to pierce

or a sinister iceberg

But then, there's Levi
with hair peaking out
from underneath a baseball hat
who smiles all teeth and dimples

who doesn't mention
that Leah is Aphrodite

but, instead,

says, *hey, we're in French class together, right?*

Votre nom est Monique, oui?

And although Monique is only my name
in our French class,
I still begin to melt.

My real name is Aster
I tell Levi

Like the punctuation? he jokes
What's it called?
An asterisk?

No, like my mother
didn't want me to be plain, I answer
somewhat drunk
I think it's a flower
My friends call me Star

You light up le ciel, Star?
he smirks
and moves
closer

and I lose all cool
become
a puddle.

8

Just as I'm about to lose myself in Levi's eyes, I hear a familiar, loud laugh. It reverberates through the small living room. *Liz.*

I think I stop breathing. No. I thought I was safe from Adam and Liz here, at this small party, this out of the way place. Why does he always show up the minute I start to forget him?

The music pulses in my ears but her deafening laughter exceeds the sound. Levi's still looking at me, apparently saying something, but I can't hear him. My feet feel cemented to the ground; I bend my knees, pull at concrete, and feign laughter. "Oh sorry I have to find my friend real quick. Be right back!" I say to him and speed walk to the other side of the house, in search of Leah. I can't find her or Melody so I text her: *Adam sighting. Hiding in the car.*

As I'm walking to the front door, someone catches my arm. I spin around. Adam. "You're avoiding me," he states, his hand still on my arm.

I shrug him off. "I am not." I shift my weight from

one foot to the other and look around the room. Liz is nowhere to be found. And where the hell is Leah?

"I think we should talk," Adam says. "I need to tell you some things."

Suddenly, the thought of sitting in Adam's car listening to his never-ending stories makes me feel angry; all of those wasted, silent moments. "I'm actually heading home now, sorry, just waiting for Leah," I say, turning my head from corner to corner, searching.

But Adam won't relent. "Mmmm, let's talk for a few minutes and then you can go home."

That arrogance. I don't miss it. "Where's your girlfriend?" I ask and try not to sound pissed. I don't want him to know how much he hurt me.

"She's...around," he says uncomfortably. "Let's go outside and talk for a minute." He takes a step toward me, and, for a split second, I consider letting him lead me away. But then I see Leah and Melody, standing behind him.

"Who invited this asshole?" Leah says, stepping beside me.

"Not me," Melody says. "I'm thinking he should get the fuck out of my house."

Adam ignores her and instead looks at Leah. "Good to see you too Leah. You know you don't have to fight Aster's battles for her. If she wants to talk to me, that's none of your business."

I'm attempting to croak out a response, but Leah suddenly yells, "Hey, Liz!" I see Liz across the room, watching us. Adam tenses. "Your boyfriend is over here trying to grab girls' asses as they walk by!"

And then Melody adds, "He's kind of a cheater, you know. You should keep him on a short leash!"

As Liz rolls her eyes and huffs away, Melody and Leah break out in hysterical laughter. Adam looks at me. "Your friends are real bitches," he says and then he's off, probably to chase after Liz.

"I can't believe he called us bitches," Leah says but she and Melody can't stop laughing. I watch them and try to smile; they did that for me, after all. But, I wish I had spoken and told him he was an asshole. I wish my voice was loud like Leah's. Why did my words get caught in my throat?

"You ready to go?" Leah asks me.

"Yea."

"Hey Aster," Melody says, "I'm sorry about Adam being here. One of my friends invited Liz. I had no idea." She looks at Leah and I can tell she feels bad. "Do you guys wanna hang out at my house next weekend?"

I'm too overwhelmed to answer.

"Levi will be there," she says and then winks at me.

"Oh, I don't know, I think I'm busy," I say distractedly.

As I follow Leah out the door, I look across the room to see if Adam's gone, but I see Levi instead. He's grinning at me and then he waves. "Au revoir, Asterisk," he yells across the room.

I feel a flutter in my chest as I smirk stupidly and wave back, but then a pressure on my right shoulder stops me cold as another voice, filled with a familiar arrogance, whispers in my ear, "I fucked up."

Before I can respond to Adam, Leah grabs my hand and pulls me out the door.

*   *   *   *

"I don't want to hear about Adam," Leah tells me on the drive home. "I want to hear about Leeeviii." She says his name like we're in a dream.

So I tell her about Levi's unexpected charm and long and lean swimmer's body even though my ear still feels warm from Adam's breathy apology, but I know for certain that's my own secret.

"He's a sophomore," she says, "and Melody says he's a math nerd. He's, like, on the math team and stuff. She's been friends with him for years; they grew up together. Did he make a move on you?"

"No! Stop, we just talked for like a second." I've only kissed one boy since my breakup with Adam, a pity kiss, from a friend who sensed my loneliness but then couldn't feign interest after I shook his hands off my body. It would be nice to be kissed romantically since Adam was always so abrupt, just like his decisive periods. And I imagine Levi's mouth might be more like the sensual curve of a question mark.

So why did I still want Adam's mouth on mine when it was so close? Why did I forget, in that intimate moment, all about Liz and the pain he caused me?

Leah waves her hands. "Okay, it's cool. He's cute. I just think you could do better."

It's after midnight and Leah drives slowly down loopy, dark back roads eluding any cops who might be on the prowl for underage drinkers. Even though Leah barely drinks, only holds one beer can for the duration of an entire night so everyone will assume she's drunk like the rest, she still likes to maintain that driving under the influence of one is still a risk.

"You don't understand," I say, as she checks her image in the rearview, always completely unaware of the spell she casts. "I don't have boys knocking down my door, like you."

But then, I realize my mistake.

"If only I could let them in," she laughs, too sadly, and I come back to the reason why she's been my best friend since grade school: we both long for the concrete parts of ourselves to change.

*   *   *   *

Leah was not always so loud; she did not always arm herself with words.

We met on the blacktop of first grade recess. After her dad left to visit his country of the Dominican, a trip that was supposed to last a few months but ended up being permanent due to issues with immigration, Leah and her mom moved a few towns over to live with family, not realizing that every single face they would see would be so white that Leah, dark like her father, would stand out everywhere she went.

Leah asked me, "Do you want to play tag?"

"Sure," I said and then, because I thought she looked different, I stupidly asked, "Why is your skin so dark?"

She looked down at one arm, inspecting it. "Oh, my mother left me out in the sun too long when I was a

baby. That's why my skin is darker than yours."
And she crossed both arms over her chest.

And in this same moment that I craved her
friendship--since she seemed lovely and
mysterious-- she turned abruptly and walked away,
vowing to never speak to me again, horrified that
this white girl would point out her obvious
differences in such a casual way.

But Leah became my best friend anyways the next
day after I pushed this boy named Liam, a third
grader, off the swing. I overheard him tell Leah that
her skin looked like the black concrete that we
played on and, even though I didn't realize what he
meant, Leah's slumped face told me the words hurt
her like a slap. Liam's cronies, a band of boys,
started to laugh, which made Leah sit on the ground
and bury her face in her hands.

I still swear that my hands barely touched his chest
when Liam tumbled backwards and hit the back of
his head on a rock, and then cried like a baby,
rocking himself back and forth, until one of the aids
came over and took him inside.

Leah held my hand as we followed the tiny drops of
blood from the swing set to the school doors so that
I could meet my punishment. When Principal Pyke
asked what happened, Leah answered first.

"I pushed him," she said, as I sat speechless in the
corner since I was a good girl who couldn't believe

that the secretary was already on the phone with my mom, detailing the account of my misbehavior. Leah looked back at me and nodded, but I was still too stunned to speak. The principal knew the real story since so many of Liam's friends had already recounted it for him, but Leah saved me from facing it all alone.

Not long after

Leah became a sort of celestial being
she grew her dark hair long
so that it just reached the small
of her back
her skin, once viewed as different
became the envy of all the girls
in our grade
who tanned for dances
and during the summer

"You're so *tan,*" they'd complain,
placing their pale arms beside hers
admiring her dark tones,
frowning at their own paleness
and unfortunate red blotches,
the only result of hours spent in the sun.

And when I'd roll my eyes
behind their backs
she'd tease me about how
I was fascinated by her skin too
True.

And even though she never owned
the power beauty gave her
remaining humble instead
I had to work hard
not to resent her
because she had everything I wanted
and never gave it a second thought.

9

On Monday, I practically sprint to French class so that I get there before Levi so I don't have to walk by him. And when he appears, half-running and breathless, I attempt nonchalance by maintaining my fake interest in *Great Expectations.*

"Bonjour Asterisk," he says and grins with pink cheeks then slides into the seat in front of me.

"Do you always wear someone else's face on your t-shirts?" I ask quickly, hoping to conceal my pleasure that the nickname stuck.

Levi looks down at Amelia Earhart (at least I think that's who it is--she's got a pilot's hat on). He looks pleased. "Ya, I do. I always wear the faces of my heroes. And a buddy of mine makes them."

During the lesson on past tense, I ignore him as best I can but smell mint and pine, a hint of aftershave, that forces me to hang on to his every movement: every slight neck stretch, every flick of his hand, every slightly bitten lip and knuckle, every scratched nose, contemplating the agony of unpredictable moments.

When the teacher tells us to find a partner, I hold my breath, wait and beg for Levi to turn around. When he does, I'm caught off guard and forget to conceal the poem I'm writing, mainly comprised of mixed up words and streams of description.

He doesn't see; thankfully he's distracted by the book of poetry on my desk called *The Trouble With Poetry.* He picks it up and leafs through it.

"Why do you write poetry?" he asks, ignoring the partner work the teacher handed us, trying to peek at the page I'm covering with hands, books, shame.

And I take too long trying to formulate a response that Levi sighs. "The trouble with poetry," he says, placing Billy Collin's book back on my desk, "is that it has no rules. Like how it can begin with one good idea but then end with some unrelated, nonsensical image? I don't get it." He frowns. "That's why I like math. There are formulas and exact answers. I mean, isn't good writing supposed to stick to the point?"

He's so serious that I laugh. "That's actually the purpose," I say. "Poetry connects uncommon things."

He pauses, looks down as he taps his pen, still contemplating. "Can it connect me to you?" he asks, with a shy raise of his eyebrow.

The Trouble with Levi

is that I can't figure out
if I should take his flirting seriously
since he jokes
with all the girls
even our French teacher
who simply rolls her eyes

So I try
not to read too much into it

Even when he leans in
and whispers
that he likes
how both of my eyes flicker green
when I smile

And, embarrassed, I glance down
at his clasped fingers
which look like tangled roots
submerged beneath trees
now strangling my beating heart.

10

After school, when I finally get a chance to check my phone, there are three separate messages from Adam.

I'm sorry.

Let's talk. When you're ready.

I'm sorry for what happened. There are things I need to tell you.

Of course I should just delete them, but his tone sounds apologetic. Something must have changed. What's the harm in hearing what he has to say? I begin typing my response but my phone rings and interrupts me. It's Mom.

"What's up?"

"Good news." She sounds breathless.

"What are you doing?"

"I'm running," she breathes heavily into the phone. "I just. *Exhale.* Wanted to tell you. *Exhale.* That I ran into Adam's. *Exhale.* Mother."

"Mom, really? Stop. I don't even care about him or his snobby family anymore." I can feel my face burn with shame. I start walking towards the school, away from crowds of students heading home or talking in groups.

Mom keeps going anyway. "Apparently. *Exhale.* Liz dumped him. *Exhale.*"

I stop walking. "*She* dumped *him?*"

"Yup," Mom sounds triumphant. "Now's your. *Exhale.* Chance."

"Chance for what Mom? I'm not getting back with him. He *cheated* on me, remember?" I say, suddenly furious.

"I know, Aster. *Exhale.* Now you can get him to want you back. *Exhale.* And then…"

"Mom, I gotta call you back," I say and hang up as she exhales a response.

I look again at the texts from Adam. No wonder he's sorry. He's alone now. Asshole. Without thinking about it further, I delete all of his texts and then, on the ride home, I tell Leah that I'm in for hanging out at Melody's.

* * * *

The next weekend on a warm afternoon me, Levi, and Leah sit around Melody's picnic table, listening to music. At some point, Melody suggests we all jump in her neighbor's pool before they get home since it's an uncharacteristically warm October day.

Immediately, I voice every excuse, specifically that I don't have a bathing suit to wear but Melody has plenty of ideas and suggests we strip down to our underwear.

I envision her abs and limbs and flawless tummy and wonder if Melody secretly hates me since she must know that my own naked body is made up of bumpy cobblestone.

Leah, sensing my distress, says, "Actually, Star hates the water. She saw someone drown at the beach when she was little. I'll go with you Melody, ok? Levi, why don't you stay here with Star? I'm sure she'd love to read you some of her poetry." And then she winks at me.

And even though I want to smack her for being so transparent, I'm so grateful that she, once again, saved my ass.

"So will you write me a poem?" Levi asks when we are alone, surprising me with his open questions, always wanting to talk more about my damn poetry. But I insist instead on the superficial stuff that will dismiss intimacy. I find out that Levi has three younger sisters, that his dad is on disability after a stroke that almost killed him, that his mom had to go back to work after being a stay at home mom for ten years in order to make enough money for them to survive, that Levi works as a swim instructor and gives his whole paycheck to his parents to help out.

Later, Levi suggests we move to Melody's semi-dark basement where it's cooler. I sit and curl my legs underneath me, but Levi's body spreads out: his long arms and legs spill out, over, across, and around the couch. He can't help it; there's just so much of him.

Eventually he changes the subject, "Do you really hate to swim?"

"No, I actually love the beach, but I do hate bathing suits," I say and force a laugh.

And he touches my knee, saying, "Maybe you just need a new bathing suit?" as if *that* is the problem. "Maybe I can help?" he says and moves his body over me so that I have to look up and I almost hook my arms around his neck to keep from tipping back. His mouth nears mine as he grabs his phone from the table behind me. "I want to show you something," he says, scrolling through it.

Levi shows me a funny video. In it, with Photoshop, they turn a hamburger into a sexy supermodel. I laugh and he smiles at me, proud of himself.

"I have a sister who hates bathing suits too."

And I know in this moment, for sure, that I want his hands exploring this body that I'm desperate to change.

*   *   *   *

With Levi, I feel, almost, okay with myself, which is so different from how I felt with Adam. At least hating my body stopped me from making one colossal mistake: I did not lose my virginity to Adam.

The first time Adam tried taking my clothes off, I pushed him off me with force. "Don't," I managed.

He smirked. "Oh, you're a Conservative."

"I'm a Democrat," I said, stupidly.

He laughed. "I mean when it comes to sex. Most girls are all over me and my friends. They want it just as much as we do. But you're different. You're guarded. I can see it in the way you dress too."

I looked down at my clothes. "The way I dress?"

"Ya, you know. You're always covered up. Like an elementary school teacher. Button down sweaters and knee length dresses? Come on. Conservative."

"I'd call it, I don't know, classy?"

"Yea, classy. That's what we'll go with...now can we take these classy clothes off so I can see what's underneath." He pulled again at my shirt, began lifting...

But underneath was not classy at all. It was rumpled. "Maybe too soon?" I answered and grabbed both of his hands. "Tell me more about that band you saw last night?"

But since Adam consistently pressured me into having sex, eventually the truth came out. We were at his house when his parents were out for the night. Adam had stolen an expensive bottle of Merlot from his parent's wine cellar. I had never had wine before, so after a couple of glasses, my head felt light and my words came out more easily.

We made out in his room for a while. Eventually, his hands groped at my body and, like usual, I made every attempt to repel them.

"What the fuck is wrong? Seriously. I get that you're not a slut, okay? Let's move this along."

I sat up, blood rushing to my face. "I don't want you to see my body," I blurted out.

I knew it was the wrong thing to say; being seen as conservative seemed, at best, charming, but admitting to my insecurity was just sad. I wanted to take it back instantly.

Adam stood up and began pacing around the room. He picked up his drum sticks. "If you hate it so much, then change it." His voice may have softened but, as usual, just declaratives. And he sounded a lot like my mother.

"It's not that easy." I pulled one of his pillows onto my lap and hugged it to me.

"Yes, it is. People lose weight all of the time. They work out. They do sit-ups."

Was he seriously trying to coach me? "I *do* work out all of the time. You know that. I'm a runner. And it's not like I eat junk food."

"But you quit track." He crossed the room to look out the window, probably to check if his parents were home. "I don't know, maybe you need a personal trainer. *I'll* work out with you."

I looked at Adam who did not seem to have an athletic bone in his body. The only sport he ever played was golf at his parent's country club. I would kick his ass on the track. "No, I don't want to work out with you. Ever."

He sighed heavily, throwing his hands up in the air. "Well, there's nothing I can do then."

I felt suddenly sober. "Just let me keep my clothes on. For now. Okay?"

Adam, instead of answering, walked over to his drum set and began banging around so that he did not have to listen to me cry.

*   *   *   *

Funny, now, with Levi, just talking about nothing in particular, I think being naked with him wouldn't be too bad, but we hear voices outside and so I get up and stretch, unsure of how comfortable I am with Melody seeing us getting, I don't know, cozy? Were we close to kissing? *Yes, definitely close.* When Leah and Melody walk through the door, Melody gives Levi a piercing look before walking quickly into the kitchen. What's her problem?

Leah follows her and Levi and I continue talking, pretending they don't even exist even though I can hear muffled voices and loud banging, and then Levi touches my leg with his hand and my body tingles. He looks shyly at me and I smile, my heart a tiny hammer in my chest.

After what seems like hours of charged silence and electric glances, Melody bounds into the room, no longer looking miffed. Levi takes his hands away from any part of my body and grabs his phone again, scrolls through his music.

Melody has on a long black dress with her wet hair pulled up in a sloppy bun. She looks like her perky, friendly self, but her shiny face and red cheeks suggest she's been drinking. Leah follows slowly behind, holding a beer, pretending to sip. I try to awaken from a trance.

Melody's music is hooked up to a speaker and soon Taylor Swift's voice floats out. Levi rolls his eyes, "Isn't there any good music on your IPod?"

Melody glares at him. "Sorry, dork, no David Bowie or Elton John or whatever gay shit you listen to."

The word "gay" hangs dangerously in the air, and I try not to look at Leah. But, unperturbed, she moves over and scrolls through the music. Eventually, and uncharacteristically, she puts on

Jay-Z and I lift my eyebrows but Levi leans back and smiles. "I like it."

The music is settled but there is a weird silence otherwise. I sit on the edge of one couch, elbows propped on my knees, wondering how I can make an exit. I give Leah a look, hoping that she'll get the hint but she just swirls her beer, looking bored.

I can't seem to bring my eyes to meet Levi's and Melody, once again, has an agitated look on her face. When she catches me glancing in her direction, she says, "Let me braid your hair," and quickly slides behind me on the couch before I can protest.

"I'm good," I say, uncomfortable and try to get up but Melody puts her warm hands on my shoulders and guides me back to my seat. "No, really, it's fine."

"Just let her do it," Levi suggests, "once she gets something in her head, it's unlikely that she'll forget about it or leave you alone."

Melody hugs me tightly from behind and whispers in a creepy, monotonous voice, "Yes, do what Melody says or you will not escape my lair." She giggles mercilessly in my ear and Levi laughs.

I give in and let Melody, while kneeling behind me, take my head in her hands. She says she want to do a goddess braid instead, after inspection, and promises that I'll love it. She asks me to face her and she parts my hair, sweeps most of my hair to the left side, scoops a large chunk from the top, and twists the bigger sections adeptly, pulling smaller strands in from the sides so that the braid will sit left to right, just in the front.

Jay-Z has finished "Empire State of Mind" and there is a pause while the next song comes on. In that moment, Melody asks me to face forward so she can finish my braid and pin it. Finally, I look at Levi, but he's not looking at me. Instead, his eyes are transfixed on Melody. He looks both enamored and saddened, like a jilted lover. I close my eyes and try to shake the thought and image from my mind.

Finally, Melody finishes my braid. She holds both of my cheeks in her hands. "You look gorgeous, baby," she says loudly and then kisses me on the cheek before presenting me to the rest of the room. Leah smiles and Levi claps.

"Let's take a picture of us," Levi suggests, sitting next to Melody and nudging Leah who comes slowly out of her silence, and we gather together on the couch as Levi extends his ape-like arms in front of us all and snaps a few pictures. When he shows them to us, I am pleased with Melody's skills. I do look pretty and love how the hair is swept out of the front of my face. But I quickly feel like a fool as I notice both Melody's and Leah's faces—how perfect they look with absolutely no effort. And then I notice Levi's other arm draped over Melody's shoulder, his long fingers dangling between her breasts. I look at me again--an incongruous face, like Leah's paintings. Nose too big, mouth too small. A Picasso.

I'd like to think I'm good enough

and believe
those things he said about me

despite the safeguards
I've placed around my heart

and then I could put my armor away
let myself lean into
the stillness of his sacred arms

let his truths about me
find their way
into all of the tiny spaces
that I may have left unguarded

but the trouble with a girl's life
is that it's unlike poetry
it does not naturally connect
uncommon things

but instead highlights
our differences
and then divides us into
deep and lonely paths of longing

11

The next week though, Levi makes me momentarily forget all about the differences between me and every other girl and instead fall in love with the word *and*. A wonderfully uncomplicated word, yet it forces a continuous conversation, and beckons my words to come out of hiding.

It's a slow day in Madame Sharpel's French class. Since we are learning words of the city life, she gives us a printout of a metropolitan area, everything labeled with French words, then puts out markers and allows us to color while we memorize the words for skyscraper, traffic, cobblestone. Levi swivels his long torso around to rest his arms on my desk. He's looking at me through eyes so eager that I have a difficult time returning his stare. He asks me question after question, but my brief responses are not enough for his curiosity. So, he repeats the conjunction with emphasis, playing seeker to my thoughts.

"*And* so when did you start your love affair with words?" he asks.

"I don't know. When I was young," I say,

pretending to be preoccupied with my purple crayon that's filling in the skyscrapers.

"And..." he prompts me, putting down a cobalt blue crayon and rummaging quietly through the brown box that we share.

The pause after that ellipsis hangs in the air, suspended, waiting patiently for my response in order to be complete. "Well, I guess I had a big imagination. I always wanted to create things. I loved stories, especially fairy tales. I wanted to be able to tell people love stories."

"*And* did you write any?" he asks, finally deciding on a bright yellow crayon to brighten up the traffic lights.

"Uh, I did, unfortunately," I stall, not wanting to bore him with the details of my childish fantasies. "I wrote lots of terrible stories that always involved love and happy endings."

He nudges my arm with his elbow. "Love, huh? Can I read them?"

"Never! Those stories are long gone," I say. I think back on the happily-ever-afters that I had conjured up in my imagination. They were never about princesses--my imagination was never that cliché. But often my protagonist suffered from some hideous ailment, like a missing ear or a disease that made her grow untouchable thorns. Other times, she was afflicted with garish nightmares or something silly like vertigo. Eventually though, she'd find someone who would fall in love with her anyways. "Besides, at some point, I decided that I wasn't any good at storytelling and so I stopped." I take a break from coloring and relax back in my seat.

"*And...?*" Levi raises his eyebrows at me, knowing there's more to the story.

"*And...*" I scowl trying to conceal my joy with frustration, "then I found poetry. And it helped me figure myself out."

"Ah, yes, poetry," Levi sighs. "Funny how the most complicated type of writing--the type that's filled with riddles--helped you to figure things out. Makes all the sense in the world."

"Well, not exactly" I say laughing. "I could take all of my real complicated feelings and thoughts and then figure them out through language. No one ever seemed to understand me, but at least I could understand things this way. It's like I had some control over that chaos."

Levi meets my long-winded answer with silence. Feeling like I've divulged too much, I pick up a crayon and color furiously.

"Huh," Levi finally says, and I realize he's just been thinking. "That's why I like math. No troubling metaphors or ambiguity. Like with poetry which is a word problem that I can never figure out. I *like* to figure things out, get an exact solution, solve the riddle. That makes me feel understood. But you'd rather muddle through metaphors." He pauses.

"*And?*" I say, teasing.

"Well, it seems like you thrive in chaos, and I find peace in the concrete systems of the universe."

"We're a bad match I guess," I say and shrug, looking down at my now colorful city. "I'm the wrecking ball; you're these impenetrable buildings."

He's silent again, frowning, and when we both reach for the same black crayon, I grab it first but he covers my hand. "Wrong," he says, taking it from me. "I'm this black crayon." He looks around the room, and finally settles on the picture in front of him. "And you're this bridge that I'm about to color in." He smirks, sits back and crosses his arms across his chest, proud of himself and his attempted metaphor.

"So are you trying to say that you fill me in? That I'm void of color without you?" I say, shaking my head.

He nods his head, slowly, proud. "It's a good start, right?"

"I mean, I guess. I wouldn't say I'm *colorless.*

And, actually why are you the *black* crayon? So, do you only add dark things to my lack of color? Wouldn't it make more sense for you to be orange or blue or green? Something that does not mean the *absence* of color. Isn't that what black is?"

"Oh ya, I'm definitely not the absence of color."

"Exactly. You better check your metaphor."

"Okay well, I guess I'll leave the metaphors to you then," he sits forward, challenging me. "But it better be about how well we mesh together."

And even though our perfect- fit comparison is at the tip of my tongue, I can't bring myself to say it out loud. "Okay," I say instead. "I'll let you know when I've got one."

"That's your homework," he says after the bell rings. "And…"

"And what?" I ask, gathering my books, feeling tingly all over, thinking about all of the color that Levi adds to my life.

But he suddenly looks down at his phone and seems, for a moment, worried. "Shit, I gotta run." He slaps his forehead lightly with his hand. "I forgot, I was supposed to meet Melody…see ya Asterisk."

And he's out the door before I can respond, leaving

me with that same conjunction and ellipsis in the air.

Of course, Melody. I shouldn't have let myself forget.

How quickly color can leave. And only its absence remains.

Metaphors for Levi

She is hurricane waves of fear
toiling at his peaceful island's shore
While his smooth sand awaits
the tender hands of a sea goddess
she creates a riptide of destruction

She is a lawless river flowing
He is the tender dam that stills
her eruptions of fantasy;
his wall always protecting
a lake he knows so well

He is the aged, fixed evergreen
she is the wind
that tugs at his branches
but he's already connected to the roots
of another's foundation

She had forgotten for a moment that

She
is
easily
forgotten

12

After school, Melody practically rams her body into Leah's car and knocks obnoxiously on my window. I roll it down slowly, "Hi?" I ask.

She's laughing and can barely answer. "Oh, hey, Leah, what's up?" she says, ignoring me. She leans her head forward, so that I have to move back in my seat, and I get an unwanted whiff of alcohol.

I'm waiting for Leah to bitch her out for acting like this; she certainly would tell me to go fuck myself if I came to school, or any place for that matter, drunk. But she just looks at her coolly and smiles sadly. "Do you want a ride home?" she asks, quiet.

"Fuck do I want that for?" Melody says sweetly and I swear Leah's going to let her have it, but she just nods instead and tells her to get home safely.

When we drive away, I stupidly ask, "Is Melody drunk? Like she's drinking at school?" I'm still looking at Leah, waiting for some sort of response. She looks in her rearview mirror. I still expect her to talk shit about Melody with me, but she stays silent. "I mean, what a loser," I say, maybe pushing it to get a reaction.

"She's not a loser," Leah finally says, a little annoyance in her tone. "She's just got a shitty life. Not everyone has a perfect life like you, you know."

"Um, wow" is all I can manage to say. *Perfect life.* That's what she thinks. In what ways is my life possibly perfect?

"Sorry," she says, quickly. "I didn't mean that. I know your life's not perfect. No one's is. It's just, I don't know, I'm just worried about her."

"Ya, I get it," I say even though I don't. If anything, Melody just brings more drama to Leah's life. I don't understand why Leah cares so much about this person who clearly only cares about herself. She didn't care about busting up me and Levi's flow; she certainly doesn't care about Leah or she wouldn't drink so much in front of her.

Leah drives on, not saying anything else. This past month, something is different about her, about us. I mean, we still drive to school together but often she is quiet, not her usual gossipy self. More reserved and constrained, like she's half-awake. I know I can't depend on her all of the time to cure my loneliness and broken heart, but she's always been there, pulling me out of dark places with her aggressive and honest nature.

"Do you wanna hang out today?" I ask her as we pull in my driveway. "We can pull up pictures of Trump and distort his face with digital images?" I say, wanting to lessen the tension.

"Um, maybe for a little bit," she says, distracted,

"but I got this big art project that I'm working on. Mr. Healey's already being relentless about building portfolios."

"Oh okay, never mind then. I should probably do some work," I yawn to prove that I'm busy too.

"Are you sure?" she asks, looking over at me. "I mean, we could definitely hang for little bit."

"It's cool," I say and gather my stuff together, hating the formality of our conversation, the politeness that is not at all familiar. "See you tomorrow."

Before I even get to my door, she's speeding off, and I'm thinking that, just like so many people in my life, she's going somewhere she'd rather be than with me.

*   *   *   *

When Leah picks me up the next morning, she's all smiles. "Hey girl," she says and I immediately breathe a sigh of relief. It feels good seeing her like that, but what brought on the change?

"You're happy," I say, questioning her.

"Just had some good coffee this morning is all," she responds. "You wanna skip school and do something more meaningful?"

"I wish I could but I've got two tests today."

Leah and I talk the whole way to school, and I'm starting to feel better about us, starting to see that, ya, we're okay. But then we pull into the parking lot and I look up to see Max and my mood goes sour. He's standing by the front door with his arms crossed and when we walk closer, he squints at us and smirks. It's like he's waiting for us. For Leah. He hasn't said anything else to her in gym class, but it's like she's always in his line of vision, and I'm always anticipating that he'll say something sinister.

Leah's talking about how so many girls in our school have the same exact shoes and backpacks. "Look," she says, pointing discreetly at the group of girls walking in front of us. "They all look exactly the same. I don't get it. Why do they want to be clones of each other?" She's so wrapped up in her rant that she doesn't seem to notice Max at all, but he's impossible for me to ignore now. As we near the entrance, he's still there, and he leans in and, real quiet, he says something that's directed at either me or Leah. I hear it so clearly, this one word: *Dyke.*

It catches me off guard as we walk through the doors but I don't stop. I keep moving, looking at Leah's face, her hands and mouth moving quickly. Did she hear him?

"Leah," I interrupt her when we are away from him. "Did you hear that?"

She stops in the hallway. "What?"

"Did you hear what Max just said?"

She looks behind her, towards the door. "Max? I didn't even see him. What'd he say?" She's so unconcerned, searching through her bag for something.

Did I imagine it? Did I put that word in his mouth? I swear he said it and his movements were so purposeful. There's no way I imagined that, right?

"Never mind," I say. There's no way I'm repeating that word to Leah.

*   *   *   *

Levi isn't in French class and, even though we exchanged numbers, I don't want to text him.

Halfway through the class, I escape to use the bathroom. I can't get Max out of my head, the way he looms, the menacing way he looks at Leah. I feel so useless, too. I know he said it, and I should have said something. I should have done something.

And what's really got me confused, more than what he said was why he said it. Does he know something about Leah? She's never told anyone, so how would he know the most offensive word to use against her?

I decide to take the long way back. As I walk down

one hallway, I see Levi. I feel a rush of happiness.
But then I see that he's not alone. He's standing by
a set of lockers talking to Melody, who is crying. I
duck behind a trophy case, hiding as if I've done
something wrong.

They are speaking in soft voices so I cannot hear
their words but their whispers and his tender tone
tell me the conversation is intimate. I inch closer,
try to pick out phrases, can see Melody clearly now,
her lips moving.

Of course she looks more beautiful sad. Of course
Levi would choose her. How foolish I was to think
otherwise, to forget that my hips are wide as the
Nile, that my thighs overlap and chafe underneath
my dress, that my eyes don't *sparkle* and my lips
aren't *pouty* and I am not, and never will be, a
fucking goddess. Point B is as far away as the
moon.

I turn on my heels and quietly walk away but can't
resist peeking back to see Levi's arms around her
while her head rests on his chest, and they are the
perfect image as she reaches her face and then hand
up, ruffles his long hair, a gesture so comfortable
and familiar that I freeze, worry my legs no longer
work.

But somehow I continue on, despite my heavy
heart.

He asked me to write him a poem

and I did write it
when my heart felt full
and his clear blue eyes
were the only thing I saw when
I tripped over things in the dark

And my lips were still tingling
from his laugh
that told me stories
and the space between his arms
fitted my words

But once the words set
themselves up on my page
the truth was revealed
in the white spaces

That glimpse into nothing
reminded me
that I always read
too much into things

Always find promise
in unspoken words

And so, no surprise
that while I wrote him a poem
hiding my true thoughts in metaphor,
hoping to remain,
in some way,
invisible

Tara A. Iacobucci

he was reading instead
the explicit poetry
of her body

13

When my alarm goes off, I can't even imagine getting out of bed and sitting in Leah's car or behind Levi in class just endlessly wondering, so I press snooze a dozen times. Eventually, Mom knocks and I convince her that I'm feeling too shitty to go to school.

"Okay, honey," she says, putting a cold hand on my forehead. "You don't feel warm, but okay. Stay home, get some rest. Call me if you need anything."

I try to fall back asleep but it's pointless. I try reading my book for English class but I'm just not interested. I try writing a poem to process all my thoughts, but words feel like heavy weights that I'm too tired to pick up. Mid-morning, I go downstairs and turn on the news.

Trump makes the headlines again, and I'm so used to this by now--seeing his face every time I turn on the TV--but this time, the clips of him fill me with a familiar anxiety. The tape of his 2005 lewd conversation with Billy Bush plays over and over. How he can have his way with women. How he can do what he pleases. The word is bleeped out, but it's clear how he feels it's acceptable to discuss a woman's genitalia.

I grab my phone and text Dad: *Did you see the newest Trump spectacle? How can he possibly defend himself now?*

He doesn't text back until his lunch break, a little while later: *He said today that it was just locker room talk. I don't know about you but that's how I used to talk in the locker room.*

Dad, gross. And no you didn't.

No, you're right. I never had time to talk about girls since I only loved my football.

I feel sick about this. How can people still want to vote for him?

Well, I hate to be the one to tell you this, but Belichick said he's voting for Trump, so now I might have to.

And I will disown you.

Well, that's fine since after Trump's elected, you women will be second class citizens anyways.

Thanks for the pep talk, Dad.

*   *   *   *

There was a time when my body felt powerful, but then words spoken had me hoping for invisibility.

In elementary school, I was the fastest girl in my grade and Tim Duncan was the only boy who could beat me in a race. I had my mother's competitive drive and my father's muscular thighs so running, or at least racing, became an easy obsession. Leah could run fast too but not like me, so she spent most of recess making bets with the boys that I would win. And I did, most of the time. Little Tim Duncan remained unbeatable though, always just a step ahead.

Junior high was when my body first began to defy me. I grew breasts and hips rapidly which impacted my running. I was still fast but not as comfortable running. Sometimes it hurt to run even with the best sports bra. I still loved to run but seldom raced on the playground anymore, preferring instead the basketball court.

But word still somehow got around about my speed because one day, in eighth grade, the high school track coach and also our junior high gym teacher, Mrs. Libertine, sought me out one day to ensure that I would be going out for track the next year. I hadn't even thought of joining a high school team but the idea of running competitively thrilled me. I told her yes and she gave me a daily workout to do to keep me in shape which I followed religiously, determined to win every single race.

Near the end of my eighth grade year, Tim Duncan challenged me to one last race. We had become friends by that point despite my frustration that he could run faster.

"Just one more run," he pleaded over lunch, as Leah and I sat eating pizza and drinking milk.

"Tim, I know you are faster than me, okay?" I huffed. "Why rub it in my face?"

Before he could answer, Leah chimed in. "I really think you can win this time, Star. Tim, did a high school coach contact *you* to make sure *you* would be on the track team next year? I think not. But one did come looking for Star."

At this point, Leah was already the object of every boy's affections, so Tim listened with keen interest. His mouth dropped. "You got scouted? I didn't even know that could happen in junior high."

"I didn't get *scouted*," I said, embarrassed. "The coach just wanted to make sure I'd try out for her team. She only has a couple of good sprinters and they are graduating this year."

"Okay, just one more race," Tim begged, "before you become a famous track star and leave us all behind in your dust."

I eventually gave in and we planned the race the following week after school. We would run the 400 yard dash, once around the track, my favorite.

On the day of the race, I had a nervous stomach but, like always, looked forward to a run, even though I would probably lose. My heart raced remembering the glory of fifth grade recess, when I had beat five boys off the line. Maybe I could do this? Leah and I walked down to the track after school and then she sat in the stands smiling and waving proudly. My biggest fan. I didn't expect anyone else to be there except for Tim's best friend, Jake, who would officiate the race but, to my surprise, three older boys sat on the grass watching us. I assumed maybe they were just there hanging out until they grinned at Tim and gave him the thumbs up. Tim looked towards them warily and gave them a small wave.

"Oh, friends of yours? Are they here to see you lose to a girl?" I joked, but Tim just shook his head. He looked nervous.

"That's my brother and his friends. I don't know why they're here," he said, "let's just do this."

Tim and I lined up, me a few steps in front since I was on the outer track. "On your mark, get set, go!" Jake yelled. I ran full sprint along the bend, sensing Tim easily catch up to my lead. He definitely improved his stride. I still stayed next to him but had a hard time concentrating on the run since, on the straightaway, the three boys had moved and were standing right next to the track, yelling *my* name. And not in the cheerful way that Leah was. "A-S-T-E-R!" they yelled slowly and in a breathless way thrusting their hips forward and back, mimicking sex.

Tim glided by me just before we crossed the finish line, winning the race. I could barely register my loss since all I wanted to do was get away from those boys. "Good race," Tim said and shook my hand, then eyed the group of boys nervously. "Let's get out of here."

We started to walk away, towards the bleachers, where Leah was waving at us, but one of the boys caught up to us. "Hey, you were right!" he called to Tim.

"Leave us alone, Ian," Tim said and then whispered, "Just ignore him. That's my brother's asshole friend." As he grabbed my wrist and pulled me along, my heart was pounding from the run and from fear.

"Hey!" Ian called louder. "I'm talking to you. Tim!"

Tim kept walking but Ian caught up to us and put his hand on Tim's shoulder. I stopped and turned around, suddenly angry. Who the hell was this kid? "What do you want?" I asked, breathless. Ian was at least a foot taller than both me and Tim. He had piercing blue eyes and a cocky smile. At this point we were at the bottom of the bleachers, and Leah had made her way down. The other two boy had also joined us.

"Tim was right," Ian went on "about your boobs. It's really amazing how you can even run with those things."

Immediately, my arms hugged my chest and Leah stepped in front of me. My guard dog. "Excuse me? What the fuck, jerk."

Ian laughed low. He gestured towards Tim. "It's just that Tim here was telling us to come see this girl run...he was going on and on about her boobs and how he's surprised they don't hit her in the face when she runs. He said they were *huge.*" He put his hand out for Tim to high five.

"I never told you to come," Tim said through gritted teeth, kicking the dirt.

"But you did tell him about Star's boobs?" Leah accused, angry, now standing over Tim. I stayed behind her, trying to disappear. "What the hell is wrong with you?"

Ian grabbed Tim and jokingly rubbed his fist over the top of his head. "Aw, this guy here. He's just becoming a man, that's all." The other boys laughed and proceeded to rough up Tim's hair.

Leah stepped close to Ian so that she was only an inch away. "You think you're cool, huh? Making my friend feel like shit so you can feel like a man? Showing Tim how to treat girls so he feels like he has some sort of power? You're disgusting."

Ian seemed to consider her words for a moment. He rubbed his chin with his hand and backed up so he could give Leah a look, his eyes crawling slowly up and down her body. "You're pretty hot for an eighth grader," he said, proving her words meant nothing. "I'm definitely going to look for you in the halls next year."

"And I'm definitely going to tell every girl I know that you have herpes," Leah shot back and then flipped him off, grabbed my hand and marched us away.

"Ya okay, you do that," Ian laughed but he sounded nervous. Then he yelled, "Thanks for the show!"

As we walked away, Tim tried to follow, mumbling about how he never asked them to come and how he was sorry. By that point, I was crying, and my face burned from embarrassment. "I'm begging you, Tim, get the hell away from me," I finally said and Tim stopped following us, walked away slowly like a wounded animal.

As Leah and I walked home, she said everything she could to soothe my pain. But I could barely listen, busy trying to piece together what had just happened. Then, it slowly registered that "the show" Ian referred to was me, my body, especially my breasts that I had already learned to cover up in large, dark t-shirts. No longer a person, but an object.

My body was no longer something I just lived in, something that sustained me. It now determined too many important things about my worth and would be the first thing everyone would evaluate before even hearing me speak.

I still ran track my freshman year; I was the fastest girl on the track, but every time I raced, I imagined all eyes glued to my bouncing breasts. The uniform shorts were tight and rode up my legs, and I constantly had to pull them down; I got rashes from my thighs rubbing together.

One day, a woman I worked with was shocked when I told her I made States. She said I did not have the body of a runner. "Your boobs are too big," she muttered under her breath. "And runners are skinny…"

One day, I stopped running for the thrill of the win and did it instead to burn calories. I ran on "bad" days, meaning days I went over my caloric limit or days I felt fat. No wonder I started to hate it and eventually quit track altogether.

One day, I began walking down the school halls with my eyes trained on the floor, entirely subconscious, and a group of older girls started a rumor that I walked with my eyes down so I could watch my boobs bounce. They mimicked me whenever I walked by.

One day, those same girls wrote mean things about my body in the bathroom stall. They etched "Aster is fat" into the door with a sharp object: such a plain, routine insult. A boy in my science class said, after he found out why I was crying, "I mean you're not *that* fat." Like that was supposed to make me feel better.

One day, in study hall, I had both hands on my head to stretch and, when no one was looking, a senior boy behind me reached underneath my armpits and squeezed both of my breasts hard. One day, I would have told someone, but, even though it lasted only a second, his virulent grip immortalized all of those other poisonous words, so that the only lasting residue was my own shame.

One day, I looked in the mirror and hated my body, so big and noticeable. If only I were smaller, thinner, flatter, I could be invisible. That was the fairy tale ending I had wished for over and over again.

*   *   *   *

When I go back to school, Levi acts like nothing has changed. He still flirts with me, asking me about what I'm writing. I don't want to tell him what I saw, and do I even have a right to? He's not my boyfriend. We're not even dating.

Leah and I drive home in silence. I feel too sad and ashamed about yet another boy rejecting me that I don't even want to talk. Leah is oddly quiet too, eyes on the road, punching buttons on the radio harder than necessary.

"I'm tired," Leah finally says as she pulls into my driveway. "I know we were supposed to hang out but can we just...not."

"Ya," I say. "No problem. But, what's is up with you? You seem caught somewhere between elation and misery for the last few weeks."

"I don't know." She pauses. "Do you think Melody has a drinking problem?" she asks. "I think she came to school drunk again today."

"I think she has a territorial problem," I answer, annoyed that this is what she's caught up thinking about. I'm so tired of hearing about her, this girl who came out of nowhere to ruin my life. I'm so mad I have to grind my teeth to stop from screaming. "Do you see the way she tries to control Levi, like she owns him. It's pathetic."

"Don't be jealous," Leah says. "Levi is definitely into you, *not* Melody."

"How would you know that?"

She pauses, unable to explain. "I can just tell," she finally says, lamely. "And, I've seen the way he looks at you."

"Have you seen the way he looks at *her*," I say,

feeling the hot stings of jealousy.

"God Star, you can be so insecure," Leah says, and the words jolt me. *Since when am I insecure? Since when does my best friend* call *me insecure?* "I know Melody is flirty and maybe seems into herself, but there's more to her than than that. I don't think people are as superficial as you make them out to be. And honestly, she's really been trying to be your friend but it's like you can't get past the fact that she's pretty."

"Easy for you to say. You've never had to worry about how you look. You've won the genetic lottery," I say, gesturing at her.

And I know this comment hurts her now even though I've said it, my own mother has said it, many times as a compliment. Leah lowers her voice and speaks in a slow, low tone that she reserves only for the boys at school who catcall her constantly. The tone that tells them their bold words of masculinity is only a cover for their every weakness. "You think my life is perfect? Jesus, I don't get to see my fucking father. Yours makes you scrambled eggs on the weekends. If my mom wasn't such a whore, then maybe I'd at least have her around. But she's a selfish narcissist. Your mom practically owns her own company and gives you whatever you want. You have no idea what you have. You're so fucking stuck up and privileged that you can't even realize that *you* have everything and I don't have shit."

"That's messed up," I say, feeling suddenly tired

and at a loss for words. "My life is a shit show." And then I think about Melody, how she ruined everything, and I feel angry all over again. "Thanks to Melody," I say, under my breath.

"Wow, it's always about you, isn't it?" She takes what seems like a calming breath, and I think she's collecting herself, maybe to apologize. But instead, she looks over and yells, "Just get the fuck out of my car!"

And even though Leah and I have never fought, have never said ugly words to each other, have been nothing but heroes in each other's life up until this point, I can't stop the comeback that's shaping in my mind from spilling out of my mouth: "At least I'm not living a lie! At least I don't hide who I am!"

And then I grab my stuff and get out of her car, slamming the door, before she can have the last word and reiterate the truth about how I am completely insecure.

When I wake up, there is a text from Levi.

                                        Hey

Hey
What's up?
I'm still mad but hoping
he will explain everything

                        Just hanging out.
Oh, cool.

                                I'm free now.
                        You wanna hang out?
                                See a movie?

Yes, all I want
is to erase one moment,
blind myself like Oedipus but…
No, I'm busy.
It's etched in my mind
a permanent black spot
of my troubles

                        Okay, busy with Leah?
                        You writing poetry today?
                                I could help.

No poetry today
Words are just shadows
that I can't hold down
I'll text you later

14

Mrs. Skye gives our class magazines and has us cut out images of women in advertisements. I'm so happy that we're doing something that doesn't require me using my brain, and I laugh since I've been doing this same activity for years. Leah and I are barely speaking. I had texted her yesterday, saying I had my dad's car for the rest of the month, and she had texted me back one word: *cool.* Maybe we just need a little break from each other. Maybe she needs time to figure out what the hell is up her ass.

When the class is finished cutting out the ads, Mrs. Skye tells us to hang them up on the front board so that the scantily dressed, passively-posed women immobilize us. We spend a silent minute shaking our heads, aching.

She has us come up with a list of what these images have in common.

"They are all thin," Mollie breaks the quiet.

"They are all beautiful," Piper says, which prompts Mrs. Skye to ask. "What does it mean to be

145

beautiful?

The words come rapidly now:

They have nice hair. Flawless skin.

No wrinkles.

Long legs.

Shiny eyes.

Toned.

Perfect teeth.

Straight nose.

Light skin (there is only one Black woman on the board).

"What else do you notice?" Mrs. Skye prompts and we get into details—about their posture, the placement of their hands. The women are passive, sexual, feminine and consequently, men hand the world to them.

Then, Mrs. Skye asks us a hard question, "How do you feel when you look at these pictures?"

Some of the girls will not say out loud, but I will see their answers later, written down on post-it notes, stuck to the board: Ugly. Fat. Boring. Not worth it. Stubby. Uncomfortable. Guilty. Finally, we begin a dialogue about the purpose of this repeated image. If it makes women feel terrible, why would advertisers use this same image of impossible beauty over and over?

It takes our class a while to see the point.

But then, the Aha moment.

I see it first, "Because they need us to feel bad about ourselves to get us to buy the product," I say.

"Yes."

"Oh, I get it now," Mollie says. "That's pretty shitty. Plus, they are all Photoshopped. That's just not fair!"

We are pleased about this discovery and we laugh about it. We laugh because we are smarter than them. We win. They lose. We will learn to accept ourselves and therefore not buy into this dangerous definition of beauty. We won't buy their products either because we don't need them now that we see our self-worth.

But that's not exactly what happens, is it?

*   *   *   *

After school, Adam's waiting for me, leaning on my dad's car. For a moment, I think how familiar he looks. I don't want to think that way, but he's got his arms crossed and his head is turned towards the sky which is sunny for such a cold, November day, and for a moment I know it would feel good to wrap my arms around him. I'm feeling so alone that I just need someone to hug me close. Adam was really good at that, even if he was terrible at everything else.

When I near him, he stands up straight. "Hi," he says.

"Hey," I say. I take out my keys but can't unlock the door since he's blocking it.

"How was your day? How are you? You look really beautiful." It's so cold that I can see his breath.

Wow, two questions and a compliment. "Thanks," I say, realizing that I have on sweatpants and a big, hooded sweatshirt. My hair is stuck underneath my winter Patriot's hat. "I'm good."

"Can we talk. Please?" he asks. "I just need to talk to you. I know you hate me but I just need a few minutes to explain." He bites his thumb nail and looks at me intently.

"I can't talk right now," I lie. "I have to pick up my dad from the train station."

"Oh," he says and looks so disappointed that I feel

guilty even though I know I shouldn't. "Tomorrow then? Or the next day," he asks and that hopeful look makes me reconsider.

"Maybe," I say. "I just really have to go now."

"Okay," he says. He takes the keys out of my hands and opens my door for me. I get in, feeling stiff. He hands me my keys and his hand brushes mine. I feel something. Is it a spark? Or just a shock of warmth after the cold?

I start the ignition and Adam taps on the window. I roll it down. "I'm sorry," he says. "For everything." And he looks so sincere, his eyes don't waver for one second; for the first time, I want to believe him.

*   *   *   *

"Election day is tomorrow," Mr. Sergi tells us. "How many of you will be voting?'

Only a couple students raise their hands, the only seniors in our class. "I wish I could vote," Max says. "This is going to be historic when Trump takes office."

I want to care about the election, but there's too much going on in my life right now. My phone buzzes and I look quickly at the incoming text. It's Adam. *Do you think you're ready to talk?* He's not giving up, but I'm not yet ready to give in. I put my phone away, swearing to myself that I'll have a final answer later.

I look over at Leah who nods in my direction. We're still not really speaking. I texted her a quick apology and she responded verbatim: *I'm sorry.* But neither of us is willing to make the next move. I definitely can't talk to her about Adam. I know exactly what she'll say, but it won't be fair. She doesn't forgive easily, nor would she understand that Adam could change and that maybe he deserves my forgiveness.

I watch her as Max continues to talk about Trump and expect her to respond. Her arms are crossed and she's definitely pissed, but her mouth remains closed.

Mr. Sergi blows his whistle. "All right, ladies to the right, men to the left. Guys, you warm up with a light jog, fifty jumping jacks, and fifty sit-ups. Ladies, same warm up but cut it in half. I have to run to the locker room. Forgot the equipment for our game today."

When he leaves, half the class does what he asks, mostly the jocks. I do the warm up and then Leah and I stand awkwardly in the center of the gym, still not speaking to each other.

After Max finishes, he moves over towards us and pretends to stretch. "When Trump's president," he says all of the sudden, "this will be a totally different America."

I don't know who he's talking to because it seems that no one's listening.

But I guess Leah's listening and gets fed up with his bullshit. "No one's going to vote for that buffoon," she says which gets Max to raise his eyebrows and smirk. "He's racist and sexist and orange. He's gonna ruin our country."

"*Our* country," Max laughs and moves in closer. The rest of the class have finished their sit-ups and now we are all together in one big group, with Max and Leah in the center.

Max looks directly at Leah and his words are sharp knives. "He will get elected, I'm certain about that. And if you don't like it, you can go back to *your* country."

What. The. Fuck.

Leah blinks twice and glares at him. Time slows. My heart pounds loudly as I wait for Leah to respond; I'm ready to back her when she does. It doesn't matter that we're fighting; she's still my best friend.

Instead, she looks right at me, her mouth agape. *Tell him to fuck off,* I think. *What are you waiting for?*
"You got nothing to say?" he mocks her. "That's a

first with that big trash mouth you got."

She walks up to him, gets really close, tries to stand her ground. He's much taller than she is. And much whiter. He looks down and whispers one word real quiet so no one else can hear, but I can hear him. And I know I don't invent the word this time: *Dyke*.

For the first time since that incident on our elementary school playground, Leah says nothing. Instead, she takes a few steps back and looks over at me like she's expecting something. Like we have something planned for a moment such as this. I'm in such shock, between his xenophobic comment and this word, that I'm just standing there, shaking my head, robbed of every word in my brain. Finally, Leah glares at me hard, like I'm the one who said it. Then, she turns on her heels and walks out of the gym.

Max laughs cruelly. "Pathetic," he calls after her. I glare at him. "You got something to say?" he says to me.

"You asshole," I say, but it's too late. It means nothing. To him. To Leah. To me. Words have power but only in certain moments. And in this particular moment, no words would assert their power over Max's hatred.

He laughs low, and I feel sick. Mr. Sergi finally runs back in the gym with two huge bags filled with basketballs. Max runs over to help him. I can't even move. Mr. Sergi starts counting us off, putting us in groups. "Where'd Nunez go?" he asks, noticing Leah's missing.

"Oh, she must be skipping class again," Max answers sweetly.

I finally find the will to move, but I have no idea what to do. I don't think there's anything I can do. I end up telling Mr. Sergi that I have cramps and he tells me I can sit out. I sit on the bottom bleacher and hug my knees to stop myself from shaking. I can't even look at Max, but I can hear him. It seems like this world belongs to him.

I text Leah the same message over and over, and this time I really mean it but know that it probably won't matter: *I'm sorry. I'm sorry. I'm sorry.*

The Trouble with Leah
By Aster Lamonte

Is that no matter how many times
we were measured
against the rest
like our backs were against the wall
with a sharpie line confirming
that one of us
was taller, thinner, better, lighter

I still saw her as the most beautiful

But how did she see herself?
I wanted to trade places
even though they teased her on the playground

and eventually she told everyone
the sun burned her skin
giving them what they wanted--
another *yes*
another slab
a willing contestant
for others to measure up to

How often we both let them determine
the parts of ourselves
that we should hate

15

Election night. Dad's glued to the television as Trump wins the first couple of states, but I can't watch. I am afraid that if sit down, I will let this sense of doom overwhelm me. Seems like no matter what happens, with this election and with my own heart, things will never be the same.

My mind keeps going back to Leah and Max. I have not seen her afraid, or voiceless, since the incident on our elementary school playground. She can always handle herself, no matter who is trying to bring her down, and I just can't understand why Max of all people has power over her.

So, to distract myself, I pace back and forth, rereading the latest text from Adam: M*eet me tomorrow. Please. I know I hurt you, and I need to talk to you in person about why. Meet me at Tops in the morning, before school….If you don't show, I promise to stop bothering you. But if you do show, then you must believe…I still love you.*

I think about meeting him. At this point, since Leah will most likely not forgive me any time soon, I have nothing to lose, besides the worst kind of loneliness.

I scroll through the pictures on my phone, inadvertently looking for Adam's face. Even though I deleted all of my photos of him, I am hoping that one was left untouched, so that I could examine what it was that made me fall for him in the first place. After going back to last year's photos, I find one of me and Leah after the Spring dance when Adam had kissed me for the first time. My eyes, because of Leah's artistic hand, do look beautiful, mysterious, smokey. Just like she had promised me. I cringe.

I think about Adam instead on that night; as always, he's a welcome distraction. I had felt so much uncertainty about my feelings towards him, but his attentiveness during a time when I felt so unwanted had impelled me to return his affections. In the picture, I am smiling and I remember the feeling I had that night, about how magic can happen in unromantic ways.

Looking at the picture of my foolish, hopeful smile, makes me remember the other moments when Adam surprised me with an affection that stirred me.

Like how he always rested his hand in my lap when he drove, making sure to adjust the radio before driving so that he did not have to remove it for the entire ride; like how he was like a Google search, and no matter what I asked him about any obscure topic, he'd have some sort of knowledge about it; like how he looked straight into my eyes before he kissed me, and his brown eyes reminded me of both solid Earth and far away galaxies; like how he always pulled me towards him when we were close and sang Coldplay in my ear.

After a couple of hours of dodging the images on TV, I finally make some coffee for Dad and sit down next to him.

"Hey kid," Dad says when I hand him the mug. "This isn't looking good."

When I look at the map on TV, it seems that red is slowly seeping throughout the states, like an endless river of blood, and my stomach drops. I sit down on the couch and hug my knees. "This can't be happening," I mumble. Dad sips his coffee and looks on with a pained expression.

Mom comes home from work late and stands beside the TV, hands on her hips, watching us, but we ignore her. "Really, you two?" she says. "You're acting like the world's ending."

"It might be," my dad says without looking at her.

"Mom, how can you not watch this? This is our future."

She shrugs, "There are more important things."

Dad harrumphs and Mom rolls her eyes before leaving the room.

CNN shows a picture of the Trump family, watching the results. Trump looks smug and satisfied, despite the stunned looks on his family's faces. And of course, here's the picture of the truth: that sometimes fairness does not win, and we often do not get what we want.

So, what do I want? The election feels out of my hands but is my heart? Is it possible to forget about the dark truth that while I swooned over Adam's voice, and his interest in me, he betrayed me? While I wrapped my arms around him, looking for a sense of belonging, he was writing his love songs for another girl.

I know that wanting to see Adam makes me weak. I know that it might even end my friendship with Leah permanently. I know, deep down, that I'm hurting from Levi's strange reversal and I'm lonely and sad and, let's face it, completely pathetic.

I stay up with Dad until 11 but he won't stop rubbing his five o'clock shadow, a sure sign that he's anxious, so I tell him to wake me up with the results in the morning and head up to bed.

I read Adam's text one more time but still can't decide what to do, so I leave it up to the stars instead of my heart. If Hillary wins, and I'm certain she will, then I know I can be strong and forget Adam for good. If she loses, I might as well hear what he has to say.

*   *   *   *

Dad wakes me up from a deep sleep with a shove. "Aster," he says, and there's an unfamiliar bark in his tone. I'm not ready for all of my conflicts, so I feign sleep. "Hey," he says louder and shakes my shoulders.

"Ya," I open my eyes and look at the clock. It's just after 5:00 a.m. Dad's smiling faintly now, so I'm thinking he must be setting me up for a joke. He will say that Trump won and laugh at my response.

And this will continue until he tires of it and finally comes out with the truth. "I don't want to know, Dad," I groan and pull the covers over my head, unwilling to give him the satisfaction of playing into his joke.

"Okay," he says sadly, and I can hear him moving away.

"Wait," I say and sit up, my stomach in knots. "*Do* I want to know?"

Dad shakes his head no. "You might just consider staying in bed today. I'd understand if you aren't okay enough to go to school."

"Very funny, Dad."

"No jokes about this, hon."

"He won?" I ask, reaching for my phone, still with a tiny hope that Dad's doing his "tell the opposite of the truth" game.

But the headlines confirm it. Trump wins.

And I lose all hope in being strong.

*   *   *   *

As I drive to the café, I feel so much anger, grief, and confusion that I'm actually looking forward to a distraction.

Adam's sitting at a table in the back corner. When I see him, I feel immobile and consider leaving before I lose all my nerve and forgive him for everything. But then I see a TV behind the take-out counter and Trump's face dominates the screen. I move forward toward Adam; anything is better than accepting reality.

"I can't believe you actually came," Adam says, as soon as I sit down across from him. His eyebrows are furrowed; he looks likes he hasn't slept much. There's two coffees on the table and an untouched, oversized muffin. "I am so, so sorry."

"About Trump?" I ask, still distracted.

"Um, no. Why, did he win?"

I stare at him in disbelief. "Seriously, Adam? Are you living underneath a rock?"

He drops his head into his hands and peeks through his fingers. "Wow, yeah. I've been so out of it lately." He reaches his arms across the table so that he's almost touching my clasped hands. "I meant I'm sorry for what I did to you. I'm sorry for messing up."

"Okay," I say slowly. "Is that all you wanted to tell me? I've heard you say that already."

"No," he says. "My parents are getting divorced."

For a few seconds, he just stares down at the table. Then he says suddenly, "Oh, I got this for you," and slides over one of the coffees. "Vanilla with milk and one sugar."

I take the coffee, trying to hide that I'm flattered that he remembered my order. "I'm so sorry," I say, confused about the timing of his confession.

"Ya," he says. "It's messed up. It's just *fucked.* They were really happy, or at least I thought they were. I don't know. I guess my mom's been cheating on him. When I found out, I freaked. And it made me scared to be with you. So I found Liz and..." His voice trails off, and I think he might cry. He composes himself and picks up the muffin in front of him. "I figured we could split this," he says, then takes a plastic knife and slices it in half. He smiles at me, like this should explain everything. "I also figured we could start over."

And as much as I want to hate him, as much as I want to remind him of how horribly he treated me, I'm just not angry any more. Disappointed? Yes. But all those angry feelings abandoned me when I look in his eyes and see, not the arrogant face that I expected, but more of a sad, remorseful boy who looks like he just lost his first championship Little League game.

"But, you cheated on me," I finally manage, "and it sucks to hear about your parents. And what your mom did is awful. It really is. But now I'm just supposed to forget about everything and trust you?"

Adam's nodding his head, "I know," he says. "When my parents told me they were splitting up, I panicked. I wanted to tell you but I was so pissed. I couldn't cope with it. But I never had feelings for Liz. And I never stopped thinking about you." He takes a small piece of the left side of the muffin and pops it in his mouth. I do the same to the other half, even though I'm not hungry.

We eat in silence. I know his parents' issues don't excuse his behavior, but at least his actions against me weren't malicious. Plus, it feels good being with him. I don't have to deal with any truths that I can't stomach, and now there's at least this explanation for his cheating which does at least warrant forgiveness.

I stare out the window and notice the leaves are still every sort of warm color: the gold ones almost glow against the cold sky, and it's beautiful, especially since winter's just around the corner. And I want to point this out to him, the little parts of things that he never seems to notice. The things that the casual passerby ignores.

"Did you sleep with her?" I ask him instead, even though I'm not entirely sure I want to know the answer.

He looks at me, his dark eyes clouding over. "Does it even matter, Aster? I love *you*. And I'll never hurt you again."

And of course this confirms my greatest fear. He did sleep with her. "How could you?"

"Jesus, Aster," he says and throws both hands up in the air. "I mean, what else can I say? I've already *begged* for your forgiveness. And I'll never even look at another girl again, okay. I've learned my lesson. You win. *You* have the upper hand, now. I thought you'd be happy." He sighs heavily. "Just forget it. I'll just leave."

"No," I stammer, "It's just..." I can feel him slipping. I don't want to get back together, I don't trust him or forgive him, but I don't want him to stop wanting me back. I lost Levi, I'm losing Leah, and the woman I thought might confirm that women can be powerful without being beautiful lost the biggest election to a man who casually talks about grabbing women's pussies.

"What?" Adam demands. He starts putting on his coat.

"I just need some time. I just need—"

But he's standing up, his face intent on leaving. He's not listening anymore, at least not like before.

I'm so scared that he'll forget me again, that I'll be back in my dark room, navigating through the glamorous lives of my peers on social media, feeling sick to my stomach and unloved, venturing down the hall into Luke's empty room, wishing hopelessly for a conversation with someone who might understand. And I think *this* must be better than that, right? Choosing the short path to forgiveness rather than the open and endless sky of loneliness.

"Okay," I say on impulse and grab his arm. "Please don't go."

He stops, looks down at me, hesitates, and then finally sits beside me. "You forgive me," he says.

"I will try," I say and attempt a smile.

He looks at his hands that are in his lap and breathes in slowly. "Okay," he says. And when he looks at me, his eyes are wet.

I put my arms around him, suddenly feeling dizzy. He hugs me back and I close my eyes and breathe into him. When we pull away from each other, he stays on my side of the table, puts his arms around my shoulder, and pulls the muffin in front of us to share. I take a bite but it's hard to swallow.

After we finish, we leave the cafe holding hands and when we pass the TV, Trump is addressing a crowd and I squeeze Adam's hand. He squeezes back and I want to feel some sense of happiness but regret takes up residence in my heart instead; the truth is that this drama with Adam will certainly not let me forget any of my awful truths. They are still there, at the tips of my fingers, burrowed deep down in my skin, and even though I know they will mercilessly be exposed sooner or later, I shrug them off like dead, autumn leaves.

I am familiar with the cold

in Austen
because it's nestled in mountains,
the chill comes in fast
and the endless falling snow
or freezing wind always numbs
hands, noses, toes.

I never really mind the snow
but the bitter air
unnerves me
when I step outside
I look around,
and see only dead limbs
and a dark, murky sky.

The mountains are mostly hidden
behind gray clouds;
only the highest mountain is visible:
a vague, blackish outline on the horizon.

Like the mountains,
I am completely lost to dark days.

{ WINTER }

16

Now that Adam and I are back together, he drives me to school. Good thing too since Leah hasn't returned my phone calls or answered my texts. I'm trying to give her space, hoping that she can realize that Max's words were not delivered from my mouth. I forgave Adam; I'm sure, in time, she'll forgive me. Luckily, today begins semester two and I no longer have gym class, so I will not have to face Max or Mr. Sergi or Leah in that space ever again.

"You good?" Adam asks as we get out of the car.

"Ya," I manage.

He smiles at me and holds out his hand. "C'mon,

I'll walk you to class."

I take his hand, even though I'm not yet ready for people to know that we're back together. Everyone probably knows what happened between us...what would they think of me for getting back with him? I continue forward, willing myself not to care.

Throughout the day, Adam insists on walking me to all of my classes, like I need a tour guide. I try to seem grateful because I know he's trying to prove he's the best boyfriend ever, but his constant attention makes me uncomfortable. As we walk through the halls, I avert my eyes from the passing crowd, pretending to concentrate on the path ahead of me. Small steps in a forward direction will certainly keep me from falling, right?

Third period. The class I have been dreading all day. Adam drops me off at French class with an abrupt kiss on the cheek that I try my best not to wipe off as I walk into the room, relieved that Levi isn't here yet. I take my seat, hoping that he's absent, but he comes in right before the bell. The person on his t-shirt today is Hillary Clinton. Her mouth is opened wide, like she's giving an impassioned speech, a small microphone right under her mouth. And even though she appears strong and heroic on Levi's shirt, I swallow the sour reality that she has become, after Trump's victory, nothing else besides the butt of a really sexist joke.

"Hey," Levi says quietly and takes a seat. No

"Asterisk," not even a French salutation. I knew it was coming, this lack of flirting, or whatever it was, but I still feel disappointed. The last few weeks I have made a pointed effort to act nonchalant. I say "hey" back and then try really hard to distract myself from looking at the dark hair on his long neck.

Madame Sharpel asks us to partner up, and before Levi has the chance to turn around, I quickly move my desk over and ask the girl next to me to be my partner. Levi gets up and works with another boy in the front of the room.

The 45 minute lesson is torture. In the silences, I swear I can hear Levi's laugh, and I want to be on the other side of it. Will every day feel like this, or will it get easier?

When the bell finally rings, Levi comes back to his seat and puts his backpack on. Before I can get out of the room to avoid him altogether, he puts both hands on my desk, stops me cold.

"Hey," he says, "Can I ask you something?"

"Sure," I say, trying to sound casual.

"Did I do something wrong? Did I mess up?"

"No, no. You didn't. Why would you ask me that?"

"It's just...I thought...I don't know," he looks at his sneakers, kicks the leg of the chair softly. It's the first time I've seen him struggle for words or confidence. "I thought we--"

Before he can finish his sentence, I hear my name. I look up. Adam's in the doorway. Of course he is. Levi looks at him, then back at me, a question now resting on his lips.

"Hey," I say to Adam and gather my stuff clumsily.

He walks over to us. "You ready?" He looks at Levi. "What's up man?"

Levi doesn't answer. He's looking at me instead, waiting for an answer. But I can't give him one.

Instead of an explanation, I say "See ya" to Levi as Adam holds out his hand to me. I don't want to take it, but I do. His hand is dry and makes my skin tingle, awaking every anxious part of me. Levi doesn't cover his shock. He actually steps back and says, "Oh."

Adam and I walk out of the room, hand in hand. I feel sick and shaky and hate myself. I hate Adam too. I let go of his hand as we stop at my locker.

"I'll meet you after school," I say. "Okay?"

"Who was that guy?" he asks, nodding back to the direction of my classroom.

"Oh, Levi?" I say. "No one really. We sometimes partner up to do work in class."

"Was he wearing Hillary Clinton's face on his shirt?" he asks, his eyebrows raised, smirking, and I nod. "That's some weird shit," he says. "What a pussy."

I open my mouth to respond. There's something important I need to say. I open my mouth, imagine a microphone in front of me, giving me some volume. I can feel my words, bubbling to the surface, so ready to be alive in the air.

But just before they can rise, Adam's arm hugs my waist and he pulls me towards him, distracting my mouth with a kiss, his tongue forcing its way into my mouth; it feels pointy and long and almost gags me. I pull back abruptly. "Love you, Star," he says, for the first time since we got back together. It's the first time he's ever called me by my nickname too. I close my eyes, searching for those words that left me during the shock of his dry lips. I fumble and, without really wanting or meaning to, I say "I love you" back. It's quiet but he hears me and smiles gratefully.

The Trouble with Adam

are those brown eyes
that make him seem impervious
to all judgments
like a child swimming in the ocean
unaffected by its cold bite
but they also remind me
how buried somewhere underneath
the shell of arrogance
is a boy
afraid of jellyfish that sting
and sharks that penetrate
long forgotten safety nets

Adam cannot be as hollow
or impenetrable as he seems

otherwise those same brown eyes
would not have that sad, tremulous light
that in some way convinced me that I mattered
at least as much as I could bear
to believe

The trouble with Adam
if I'm being honest
has more to do
with the trouble with me

17

Mollie slides her notebook on to my desk during a partner activity on compassion. "Hey," she says and I try to smile back at her.

We are supposed to read a poem by Maya Angelou called "Phenomenal Woman" and then explain how the poet's self-compassion gives the speaker power over her thoughts. *Phenomenal Woman.* No wonder why boys don't take Mrs. Skye's class. I wonder if she chooses these types of poems for that exact purpose.

"So many of you are writing about the things in life that pain you, the words that tie you down," Mrs. Skye explains, "but I think it's important for all of you to see the impact of positive words, to see how words can actually create thoughts in our own minds, and how thoughts shape, not only how we feel about ourselves, but also how society views us. I think everyone in this room could benefit from more self-love in our lives and in our writing and then our audience will recognize the power we hold in spite of the struggles we face." I swear she looks right at me when she says this. I look down at my hot palms. Sometimes I wonder if she was really supposed to be a therapist.

Mollie puts the copy of Maya Angelou's poem on my desk and rests her elbow there. "You seem really down," she says, "you okay?"

I think about lying but then I notice that, when Mollie moves her head to the side, she has a chunk of hair that is dyed a dark purple which hides like a child's worst kept secret. I decide to speak just one truth. "Not really. Adam and I got back together." Mollie is shading in a flower that she has drawn on the top of her notebook. It reminds me of an Aster flower, with long petals and a dark middle, like a firework. She raises her eyes at me and frowns. "I think I made a mistake."

"Girls, let's get to work," Mrs. Skye says gently from behind us.

Mollie draws her face down, all serious and reads out loud to show Mrs. Skye we're working:
"Pretty women wonder where my secret lies.
I'm not cute or built to suit a fashion model's size
But when I start to tell them,
They think I'm telling lies."

When Mrs. Skye moves away from us, Mollie leans down and whispers, "Why do you think you made a mistake?"

"I just don't know how I really feel. Sometimes I know I want to be with him, like we had a good thing before he cheated on me. At least I think we did. It's like I can't even remember."

"Asshole," Mollie says too loudly and gets a stern look from Mrs. Skye across the room so she reads,
"I say,
It's in the reach of my arms,
The span of my hips,
The stride of my step,
The curl of my lips.
I'm a woman
Phenomenally.
Phenomenal woman,
That's me."

Mollie pauses and raises her eyebrows at me. I continue. "It feels good, mostly, when we're together. But, then, I mean, he doesn't always do or say the right thing. And, when we're not together, I have a bad feeling, like a sense of doom. But I don't know if it has to do with him or just with me."

Mollie underlines some lines in the poem as I talk. I continue, telling her about Adam's parents, Liz, the election. I leave out anything to do with my body, my mom, my issues with pretty.

"What part shows compassion?" I ask when Mrs. Skye tells the class we have one minute left.

"How about this:
I walk into a room

Just as cool as you please,
And to a man,
The fellows stand or
Fall down on their knees.
Then they swarm around me,
A hive of honey bees.
I say,
It's the fire in my eyes,
And the flash of my teeth,
The swing in my waist,
And the joy in my feet.
I'm a woman
Phenomenally."

Mrs. Skye brings us back as a whole group to read
the poem together. She reads it slowly,
lingering on the positive words, and I really try to
listen closely to the part where Mollie and I
left off:
"Men themselves have wondered
What they see in me.
They try so much
But they can't touch
My inner mystery.
When I try to show them,
They say they still can't see.
I say,
It's in the arch of my back,
The sun of my smile,
The ride of my breasts,
The grace of my style.
I'm a woman
Phenomenally.

Phenomenal woman,
That's me."

Mollie has written me a note on the top of the page:
Adam doesn't deserve you. I stare at it, trying to let
the words soak in.

Mrs. Skye must notice that I'm not paying attention.
She makes me read the last stanza aloud.

I read it slowly, contemplating the irony.
"Now you understand
Just why my head's not bowed.
I don't shout or jump about
Or have to talk real loud.
When you see me passing,
It ought to make you proud.
I say,
It's in the click of my heels,
The bend of my hair,
the palm of my hand,
The need for my care.
'Cause I'm a woman
Phenomenally.
Phenomenal woman,
That's me."

When I get to the end I notice Mollie has circled
"Phenomenal woman" and then crossed off
"Me" and written "you" with a smiley face. I look
over at her and she smiles wide, gives me two
thumbs up. I feel a little lift in my spirit as the class
shares their thoughts on self-compassion

found in the poem. We then talk about how her own
compliments must lift her up as a human
and a woman, especially a woman of color. She has
decided she's worthy of love, and her words
are a testament to that truth. It seems so simple, yet I
know how difficult it is to speak to myself
with any sort of kindness.

"I am going to give this class an unusual homework
assignment," Mrs. Skye says after we wrap up our
discussion, and before we can complain about how
much work we have already, she holds up her hand
to silence our groans. "It will not involve reading
or writing."

We still all groan again.

Mrs. Skye continues, explaining that this one is
personal and important, one we never learn in
school: it's about self-compassion. "There are two
parts," she explains. "First, you have to look at
yourself in the mirror every day and say something
nice about how you look."

We snicker.

She raises her eyes, "Then, I want you to say
something nice to yourself about who *you are.*"

Now, we roll our eyes, but she looks so serious, so
caring, that we don't dare tell her how impossible
these things will be for us. We all nod our heads
instead.

"We've talked so much this year about how words are powerful, and the words you speak to yourself shape your core. They can hold you prisoner or they can set you free."

I think about the wicked Queen's mirror from *Snow White.* Would Mrs. Skye think that her glimpse into the mirror was about self-love and not wickedness? *Mirror, Mirror on the wall. Who is the fairest of them all?* Once upon a time, the Queen believed herself to be phenomenal until it showed her someone better. Was it this comparison that stole all of her goodness and joy?

Mrs. Skye suggests we look at ourselves through the eyes of someone who has only compassion for us. Someone who would never hurt us. Someone who loves us unconditionally and sees the good, and even loves the bad. "And then, of course, you'll journal about this new experience."

Mollie raises her hand. "Mrs. Skye? What if this *isn't* a new experience for us?"

"What do you mean?" Mrs. Skye rests her hand on her chin, a sign that she's really interested in the question. She loves Mollie.

"Well, I already say nice things to myself every day. Actually, I've been doing that for years." Mrs. Skye and most of the class laugh. "What?" Mollie looks around. "You guys don't?" And despite that little sense of doom I can still feel in my heart, I laugh.

*   *   *   *

When Luke and I were younger, once a year Mom would let us skip a full day of school and she would take us shopping or wherever we wanted to go. Luke obviously just wanted to stay home and do nothing, but Mom forced him out of the house, committed to having fun with him for at least one day. I don't really know what they ended up doing, probably shopping for comic book collectibles. Unlike Luke, I reveled in this solitary day with Mom, and always looked forward to that moment during the year when she had me pick out my special day.

I'm thinking of this lately, of how much I want to escape back into the safety of my mother's arms and be this perfect daughter that I used to be, before my body grew and deceived me.

So I complain relentlessly to my mother about how stressed I am at school and it only takes her a week to suggest we play hooky the next day and visit her gym. "We can work out at the gym, then get lunch and go shopping?"

I always avoid doing a work out with mom, since her strength and agility put me to shame, but I know she won't agree to skip out on a chance to exercise on a day off, and anything sounds better than dealing with Adam, so I say sure.

Mom lets me sleep in and then she makes us protein smoothies and packs a gym bag full of waters and towels.

"Are your shorts a little small?" Mom says when I walk into the kitchen.

"I know," I say.

I hope to drive to the club in silence, but Mom's wide awake and full of energy. "What's going on with you and Leah?" she asks. "I haven't seen her around for weeks."

"I don't know," I answer. "We're just not getting along right now."

"You two *never* fight. *Something* must have happened."

She's right. I think back to how close we were growing up. After that terrible recess incident, we became inseparable, so much that we demanded, pretty much every year, that we celebrate our birthdays on the same day even though we were born a whole month apart. But it was one exact month, both of us being born on the 15th, and we figured that we were twins of some sort. I still have the picture of us when we turned nine in matching outfits that we begged my mom to buy for us: pink and gray striped shirts with gold lettering. My shirt said "best" and hers said "friend." We wore our hair in side ponytails--hers to the left and mine to the right. Leah had put makeup on me for the first time and so my cheeks looked sweaty. Our arms wrapped around each other, we smiled into the camera like two pageant winners. Was this the first time I noticed that, even though dressed exactly the same, we could not look more different?

"It's not over a boy, is it?" Mom asks.

I hold back from telling Mom that Leah's gay. Not because she'd care, but more because it's the only connection I have to Leah, and I won't throw it away on a whim. "Definitely *not*," I say instead. "Adam and I got back together. You know how she feels about him. She's just bothered by it," I lie.

"I told you he'd come crawling back," Mom says and smiles over at me, her eyes hidden behind her large sunglasses that she wears even on sunless days. "You didn't have to get back together with him, though."

I close my eyes and will her to stop speaking. "Ya, well, we're good."

"If you just-"Mom starts.

"Can we *please* stop talking about it now," I almost yell, desperately needing to stop any of her advice from reaching my ear. "Everything's fine Mom."

At the gym, we take a cardio weightlifting class that makes me sweat in the first five minutes. The room is full of women only, and the instructor talks non-stop when she's not yelling at us to kick harder. She also keeps yelling at us to "Smile!" I'm finding it impossible to smile between the grunting.

Halfway through the hour class, the instructor gives us a two minute break to get some water. "You're doing great!" Mom says, not the least bit out of breath. I feel like I might vomit.

"Ya," I say and sip my water.

My mother's gym friend, Grace, comes over, saves me. She is a lovely woman with a full head of gray hair, kind smiles, and good energy. I haven't seen her since the summer. "Hey, Aster," she says, "You look great!" She grabs both of my hands and squeezes them. "How are you?" Then she looks at my mom, putting an arm around her shoulder. "Gina, your daughter is absolutely radiant!"

The compliment embarrasses me; although it's genuine, it's not the least bit true.

Before I can answer, my mother responds, "She does look good! I mean every girl gains a *little* bit of weight when they reach this age. But she'll thin out soon, like I did."

My mother looks at my body that I can't hide and throws her arm around my shoulder; then she laughs like we're sharing our favorite joke. Grace stands by, unsure of how to massage the tension.

I'm rescued by the instructor who is yelling at us again to smile through the rest of the workout. Our two minute break over, my mom puts down her water and picks up her weights. Grace waves at me sheepishly and crosses the room. I'm so stunned by my mother's words that I can't seem to move. I stand there stupidly while all the bodies press their weights around me. I finally manage to pick up my ten pounders which feel so much heavier now, like they're nailed to the ground.

Eventually, I stand in front of the mirror that takes up the entire front wall. For the rest of the hour, my eyes see my mother--her slender body, her strong arms--and me--my teapot hips, my trunk-like thighs. I think about the irony of Mrs. Skye's assignment-- how could I speak nicely to this reflection that so clearly points out my every flaw?

Mirror, Mirror on the wall...

I try to conjure up a positive word but immediately my brain thinks, *disgusting.* And there's more: *Fat, prude, boring.*

I say it all to my mirror image. *Not the fairest at all.*

Mrs. Skye is wrong. If I hate myself enough, I can force myself to change and then maybe I'll love myself.

You're disgusting. I say.

I catch the instructor's eye just as she says, "smile!"

I meet my own eyes; they are not smiling; they only see what's clearly there.

You're Disgusting. Disgusting. Disgusting.

        *   *   *   *

Once upon a time, Luke, Mom, and I spent almost every weekend during the summer at the beach where I learned to wish on waves because wishing on stars was too cliché. We'd leave early in the morning, before the crowds came, pack lunch and drinks in our cooler, then drag boogie-boards, fold-up chairs, and a bright blue umbrella through the sand to a spot near the water. Mom glistened in dark tanning oil, her darker skin able to take the heat of the sun, while she lathered Luke and me in SPF 50 which had to be reapplied every hour or so.

Mom would tell Luke to bring me into the water and watch me closely, and then she'd lay on her belly, shut her eyes, and let the sun warm her skin. Luke would only put his tippy toes in the water, then complain about the frigid temperature while I dived in and rode the waves. "You're okay, right?" he'd ask me. "Don't go too far and make sure Mom is always in your sight," he'd say and then I'd float on my board, watching him go until he was just an unrecognizable shape in the distance. I'd come up from the water and beg mom to swim. She would come in sometimes but only to her waist and yell "watch out!" every time a big wave surfaced in the distance and then she'd jump as high as she could when it reached her. She hated getting her hair wet. Eventually, she'd mosey back to her chair, leaving me to navigate the waves alone. When I could no longer stand my wrinkled hands, I'd sit next to her on my own blanket and open the cooler; she always packed it full of healthy snacks.

Once upon a time, when I was ten, I took off my shirt, ready to sprint into the water and submerge myself until my entire body pruned but mom looked at me funny. She stared at my belly, her eyes pinched together, the same face she made before assessing if my skin had turned any shade of pink and needed more sun block.

"Honey," she said, sucking in her breath. "What have you been eating?"

I looked down at my bright pink one piece bathing suit, my favorite. Was my belly making a bump now? I sucked in my gut and looked up at her, shielding my eyes from the bright sun. "Why?" I asked.

She took a big breath in, so loud that I could hear it, bent her knees so that we were the same height, and pinched my waist. "It's just--" she began but then dropped her hand to her knee. "Nothing."

"What Mom?" I pleaded, but she was already moving towards her chair.

"Nothing honey. Really. Go play. Luke's already in the water." She sounded tired.

Once upon this particular time, after Luke's body

had become invisible, I lay on my board and let myself drift a little far out in the ocean letting the waves rock me, concentrating on one single wish.

I'm not sure how long I zoned out for, considering words like *fat* and wishing, for the first time, that I could change my body, but at some point, I looked up and could not find my mother. I panicked and swam to shore, then ran up and down the beach, gasping for breath, my mom's umbrella nowhere to be found.

For a few minutes, I sat in the wet sand near the water and let myself cry, figuring I would never find my mom again, thinking how maybe I deserved this. I took deep breaths the way mom taught me, and eventually calmed down enough to remember how Mom had told me once that if I ever needed help, find another mom. "Find a woman with young kids. Moms will always help," she had said.

So, I took steps around a small circle, looking for a Mom. There were a lot of them at the beach that day, so I tried to find one that looked like mine, believing this would be best. There was a woman building sandcastles with two small children who had dark hair and a friendly smile. I walked and stood behind her. "Hi," I said quietly. She didn't respond, so I tapped her on her shoulder.

"Hey," she said and smiled.

"I'm lost," I said and then began to cry again.

"Oh, honey," she said, and sat down beside me. "Were you with your mom?"

'Ya," I sniffed.

"What does she look like?"

I described my mom and our blue striped umbrella. She brought her two children back up to the blanket where a man was sitting. Then, she took my hand and we walked slowly down the beach, the way I hoped my mother would be.

My mother saw me first. "Aster!" I heard her yell and when I turned, she was running towards me. When she neared me, she wrapped her arms around me and fell on her knees. "Thank God!" she kept repeating in my ears, her body cold and wet. I could almost taste the salt on her and knew she must have been in the water, looking for me. I felt even more ashamed. Why couldn't I look how she wanted me to look? Why didn't I do what she wanted me to do?

Mom thanked the woman over and over for helping me and then walked me back to our spot, which was not too far away. Our umbrella seemed taller than everyone else's and more colorful, more vibrant in the sunlight. I'm not sure how I had lost track of it in the first place.

When we got back, we sat on the blanket together, facing each other. I couldn't stop crying, even after she made me drink water and take deep breaths. Finally, she took my face in the palms of her hands and looked at me closely. "You're okay," she said.

"I'm sorry, Mom," I said, wiping sandy tears from my face. I was sorry for so many things.

"Aster, no! I should have been watching you. I shouldn't have trusted Luke. I will never let you out of my sight again. *I'm* sorry."

In that moment, when my chest relaxed from the released anxiety and those first feelings of shame for not being what my mother wanted, and I could rest my head in her lap, I knew for certain that my mom loved me...and everything felt perfect, so perfect that I have tried too many times to recreate that moment we shared. Maybe I should have worked harder at getting her to let go of me since sometimes her grip that protected me was loving but also toxic: her eyes that were always trained on me often trapped me in her sun's rays and burned my ultra-sensitive skin.

The Trouble with My Mother
By Aster Lamont

Is that she has never yelled at me
not ever
not even when I spilled orange juice
in her *Coach* bag
ruining the contents inside
not even when I got caught
shoplifting once at Wal-Mart
or drinking in the woods my freshman year

And even though
she always says the wrong thing
always hurts me
in my most vulnerable moments
always reminds me
simply by her presence
about my failures

she believes her words
will guide me
to a better life
believes my insecurities
will drive me
to work harder
believes thinness
will allow me
to feel
powerful

And when I give her my poem
to read, she asks

what I ate for breakfast
how many grams of sugar
in my bowl

I tell her the title
is a hint at the message
and the metaphor is easy to understand
if you were paying attention

She asks if I worked out
how many calories
stored and burned
I tell her that the imagery
should remind her
of the hidden fears of a young girl
obsessed with an impossible quest

And even though
we are reading
two very different poems
I still consider her analysis

I know hers is wrong
so why do I still believe her?

18

Nearing the end of winter, when I no longer miss the warm sun on my arms or the green leaves on the trees because the gray sky and icicles feel permanent and familiar, and when the loss of Levi's affections becomes almost a blessing since at least I no longer yearn for his attention so much that my chest hurts, I walk into school and am confronted by Leah. It's not her exactly, but a painting by her that is displayed in the main hallway of the art wing.

It's different than her others--it's a female in the center, that's clear, but everything seems proportional: no uneven body parts or monstrous features. Although it's difficult to see the face due to a ribbon wound around her from crown to chin, it still does not feels like authentically Leah. Underneath is a quote from Audre Lorde: "Nothing I accept about myself can be used against me to diminish me." I double check the name at the bottom. *Leah Nunez.* The painting is so beautiful I can't even look at it without feeling that familiar longing--once again, Leah feels so far from my reach just like every wish I have.

As if the day isn't bad enough, Mrs. Skye keeps me

after class to discuss my work.

She actually sits at her teacher's desk, which she never does, so I stand awkwardly in front of her, hugging my notebook. I can see that she has a stack of student writing on her desk; my poem, I think, is on top. "What's up, Aster?" She stares at me, slightly frowning.

"Am I in trouble?" I ask her.

"No, of course not," she answers quickly. "I just wanted to tell you how much I enjoy how your poems have a recurring theme. *The Trouble With...*It's a really cool concept."

"Thank you," I say slowly. "I got the idea from one of my favorite poems."

"Really cool. I also wanted to talk to you about this one." She holds up the last one I wrote about my mother. "Well, the assignment asked you to use the same theme of self-compassion as Maya Angelou's poem. Remember that work that we did in class?" I nod. "You didn't exactly follow the directions, so I wanted to give you a chance to revise."

"Okay, so you want me to add in something about self-compassion?" I ask, taking the poem from her.

"Well, ya, sort of. Also, you started off the year so strong, but lately, I don't know, I feel like your writing is less honest and because of that it's become too basic."

"What do you mean?"

"Well, take this poem. It talks about a poem that you give your mother, but I think I'm more interested in reading *that* poem than *this one.* It's like you took the easy way out--talking around the metaphors instead of working through them. I mean, I know that writing about personal things can make us feel vulnerable, but that's also when artists are able to create the most beautiful works of art."

"Oh," I say, looking away from her, thinking about Leah's painting and knowing that it must be a result of her personal struggles, and I have no idea what it means. Does that mean I've lost Leah for good? "I'm really trying. I guess I'm just...I don't know...it's just been a tough year." I know Mrs. Skye is just trying to help me, but her words hurt. I repeat the quote from Leah's painting in my head several times, trying to block out Mrs. Skye's honest voice: *Nothing I accept about myself can be used against me to diminish me.*

"Aster, I know that you're trying. And it's very difficult for me to assess someone's poetry since it's usually highly emotional and projects how a poet is feeling, and of course this type of assessment is always subjective. But I've seen what you've done, and I hear what you say in class, and I just think you have more to say than what is on the surface."

"Okay," I say. *Nothing I accept about myself...*

"I don't want to upset you or make you think you don't have talent. You do, believe me. I just want you to dig a little. I don't want you to settle for the simple. That's not who you are." She holds out my poem and her black ink drips dark around my words. "You okay, Aster?"

"Ya, I'm good," I lie. *Can be used against me...*

"Aster," she says, so loudly that I fully come back to her voice. "So, I'd really like you to revise this, okay? Just think more about the conversations we've had in class about word choice and impact. And reflect on what you're struggling with but also how you have power over that struggle because you've named it. Once you name it, you can overcome it."

"Sure," I fake a tiny smile. "When's it due?" *...to diminish me...*

"When you're ready," she says. "Take your time with it. Just promise me that you'll spend some time reflecting on what you really want to say." She smiles up at me, and I try to mimic the movement with my own mouth but end up just clenching my teeth.

In the hallways, I read the comments. In the margins, beside my poem, are suggestions from Mrs. Skye, stuff about extending my metaphors and strengthening my imagery, more show, less tell. I barely read them, too embarrassed by the truth that I'm probably just not a capable writer and maybe mom was right and I should look at another career. I don't know why I ever thought I could write. It seems that the only thing I'm consistent with is failing at everything and so I crumple up the paper and throw it in the trash. *Nothing I accept about myself can be used against me to diminish me.* What if that one thing I accept about myself is that I'm worthless?

Before I leave, I return to Leah's poster and stare at it hard. If I had seen this months ago, I bet I could have understood it better, but today I don't know the context. I take a picture of it on my phone because even though the warmth of the sun is beginning to slip from my memory, Leah is all I see when I regretfully close my eyes.

*   *   *   *

I don't come downstairs Saturday morning even though Mom calls my name multiple times. She comes up to my room around noon, but I tell her to go away and turn my face towards the wall. She doesn't protest; she has a work meeting in the city anyways. When I'm certain she's gone, I go downstairs and make coffee. Ever since our day off at the gym, I've been doing my best to avoid her.

Dad's watching college football and pats the seat beside him. "C'mere," he says, gently, and I am finally swayed.

"Hi," he says, after I sit down but then turns his attention back to the game.

I sigh heavily, hoping he'll get the hint.

"How's school?" he asks, an innocuous subject that he can ask me, not expecting any complicated answers.

"Okay," I say.

"Mmmmm…" he says.

We watch the rest of the game in silence, and a failed hail Mary pass that makes Dad cringe. "This team always lets me down," he says. The final score is 26 to 20. He shuts off the TV.

"Dad, do you think maybe I should quit writing?" I ask. "Maybe do what Mom does instead?"

"What does Mom do?" he asks.

"I have no idea," I say. "Something in an office, bosses people around I guess, makes people do stuff for her. Is that what she does?" Now that I think about it, I'm not entirely sure what she does when she's outside of our house.

"I have no freaking clue," he says and we both laugh. "Honey, why would you ever want to give up writing? You've been rhyming since you could talk."

"Dad, my poems don't *rhyme.*"

"I know Aster. I was just being, you know, hyperbolic." He raises his eyebrows at me. "Yeah?"

"Good job, Dad. *Anyways* I don't know. Do you think I'm any good?" I try not to put all of my hope in his answer.

"I mean, I don't understand a word you write," Dad says and smiles at me proudly, "so it must be good then, right? Good writing uses a lot of those big words, and describes things in a way that you have to think about real hard. What's that called?"

"Figurative language?" I say.

"Ya, language you have to figure out. Right?"

"Sure Dad."

"Okay, so ya, keep writing stuff I can't understand and I'll keep pretending I know exactly what you mean. It's a fun game that we've always played."

"That's the thing, Dad. You and mom aren't writers. I mean, usually writers breed more writers. Where did I come from then? And I hate that you and mom don't understand me. I mean, I get that *you* try, but she never reads anything I write."

Dad rubs his beard, thinking. "Yea but who cares? None of my immediate family are carpenters. Come to think of it, my old man couldn't even fix a leaky faucet. And your mom? Her father lifted heavy boxes all day at a factory and couldn't lead a horse to water. But look at your mom. She's the boss now."

"I guess," I say softly.

We sit in silence, listening to the house creak from

the cold wind outside. I don't know what I expect him to say, but I still wait for the words.

"And you know what else you're good at that your dad can't do?" Dad asks, nudging me.

"What?" I ask.

"Making sandwiches. Now, go on and make me one now. I'm hungry after all this smart talk." He rubs his belly.

"Make it yourself," I say, punching him in the arm. "If there's anything I've learned from Mom, it's that I'm not to live my life waiting on some man. And make me one too, while you're at it."

"Okay, my queen," Dad says and stands up, stretching. He looks down at me. "You okay?" he asks, and it's so out of character for him that I impulsively answer yes.

*　　　*　　　*　　　*

Later, I'm up in my room, staring at a blank computer screen when Dad knocks. He peeks his head in. "I have something for you, but you can't tell your mother."

"What?" I say, getting up and opening the door. He hands me a folded piece of paper, a little wrinkled and yellowed with age. "What is it?" I ask, taking it from him.

"Your Mom wrote it for me, after I proposed. She gave it to me on our wedding day." I look down to read it but he covers it with his hand. "Wait, not until I leave. I have a feeling you're gonna get all sappy. And I feel bad about it now. I never told her how much I loved it. But I did love it, and I understood every word."

"Wait, Mom used to write?"

"A little bit. She dabbled I think. When she was young. Not like you though."

"Oh," I say, holding the paper gently, afraid of ruining it. "Thank you."

Dad smiles sheepishly and leaves.

Here are my mother's words:
A quiet night—with firelight
We've talked away the hours
Simple dreams, and it just seems
Love has many powers.

Some honest talk, a little walk,
We've learned so much today;
How much I care, when you are near
And love has found a way.

A warming mist, my lips are kissed,
We walk along the beach;
Our wants, our needs, are simple seeds
Which put love within our reach.

A glass of wine, your hand in mine,
We promise our love forever.
Bright stars above, a night of love
That has brought us together.

A choir to sing, a wedding ring,
The beauty of a dove
The time is now, to take the vow,
And live our life in love.

I fold the paper as many times as I can, unsure of what to do with her words. I don't know what surprises me more: that my mom wrote poetry or that she never thought to tell me. Or that she was so, I don't know, *romantic?* My mother, not a villain or a hero but a writer?

I know this discovery should make me feel somewhat happy or at least satisfied but all I feel is alone. If anything, this just makes things more unfair. If mom wrote, why wouldn't she tell me? Why wouldn't she try to make this connection between us transparent? Why wouldn't she have supported me more when I talked about my dreams of being a writer instead of encouraging me to be pretty above everything else?

To distract myself, I open up my phone and stare at the screenshot I took of Leah's painting and try my hardest to make connections between all of the things that I don't understand.

*   *   *   *

When Adam asks me to come over his house on Friday night, I know what he wants us to do. He subtly mentions that no one will be home, and so of course I know what he's planning. And even though

I still am not ready, I agree. I concede. I say *yes* because that's all I can do lately to keep from sinking into a bitter misery. Pleasing others has always been my strength. Affirmative words roll so easily off my tongue, while *no* takes too much effort, so I bury my concerns underneath my smile and throw dirt on it.

I drive over in Dad's car, blasting Drake's raps to drown out any thoughts of doubt. I've always loved to think, to dwell on things, to let thoughts swirl in my mind like funnel clouds, but lately I've just yearned for a blank canvas of thought. Whenever I do start to think about my mom's poem, or Leah's painting, I just get frustrated. At any other time in my life, I would put pen to paper and free myself from my tumbled thoughts by writing; poetry always led me to a destination, like a map. But whenever I try to write, Mrs. Skye's criticism stops me short, snaps my pen in half. If nothing else, Adam continues to be a distraction from my untidy mind that has stopped connecting uncommon things.

I let myself in through the big, oak door that always looks heavier than it is. Adam has turned on every light in his large house. I let myself linger in the foyer, the smell of garlic and tomato sauce calming my nerves. Adam isn't the greatest chef, but he can whip up a reasonable pasta dish without effort, a skill he learned from his live-in nanny when he was young.

"Hey, is that you?" he calls from somewhere upstairs, his loud voice echoing down the stairs. "Be right down."

I sit on the couch in the living room and flip through his mom's bridal magazines; women dressed fashionably in corsets and flowing, white gowns grace the covers. They are mostly bunching up their dresses and looking off into the distance or else glancing behind them, I guess at their happily-ever-after. I end up placing them face down in front of me, so that I can only stare at advertisements for wedding venues and flower shops, the pictures luckily devoid of any characters.

Adam finally makes his appearance ten minutes later even though he told me to be there at 7:00 p.m. sharp which was almost an hour ago. He has gelled his short, military, cropped hair and put on strong cologne that reminds me of Mr. Sergi. I grimace while trying to smile. "Hey," I say.

He takes a seat on another couch, his arm slung around a large pillow. His distance makes me hesitate, as always. Why isn't his most comfortable space the one beside me?

"I made us dinner," he says.

"Okay." I feel like I'm stuck in a black and white movie, the subtitles mocking our awkward dialogue.

We eat at the high top table in the kitchen and

Adam serves me a bowl of spaghetti and pours me a glass of red wine even though I don't ask for one. I drink it down before I even take a bite of my pasta while he rolls a joint with meticulous, deft fingers. He talks about his parent's divorce, how his dad is staying at a friend's house until they figure things out, how this weekend they went on separate vacations for the first time and he wonders if his mom went with her new boyfriend. "Fucking bitch, right?" he says. I nod sympathetically and frown at all the right pauses but feel next to nothing. I can only think, nonsensically, *let's just get this over with...*

So, finally, when Adam asks, during a movie he puts on that night, a boring history film about ancient civilization that neither of us are really watching, to massage my shoulders, I say *sure.* When he moves his hands from my shoulders to my breasts and kisses my neck ever so gently, I nod my head. When he whispers in my ear to come upstairs with him, I take his hand willingly, and calm the voices screaming *no* in my head by placing one foot in front of the other and pretending that this is exactly what I want, placing even more dirt over any complicated thoughts to bury them deeper.

Adam's bedroom is spotless and smells like Lysol. He lights a sage candle and turns off the light--one part of the night I happily concede to. We are both silent as we pull back the covers. *Yes* I think as I lie down, making sure to stretch out my belly flat like I'm rolling out dough. *Sure* I think as Adam slides off his shirt and I put both palms on my own chest to calm my breathing. *Why not?* I reason as he moves his hand to my waist and then down to the top of my yoga pants. And it almost even feels good but like always my mind is too present, not a blank canvas at all but a factory of bustling activity, the dirt thinning, revealing the truth hidden underneath. I can't stop thinking about so many questions that are always there in the back of my mind: What would Leah say to me in this moment? How much will I hate myself in the morning? Will my naked body repel him?

And as I close my eyes, which Adam takes as an invitation to maneuver his body on top of me, I suddenly remember: *Liz.* The sound of her raucous laugh intrudes upon my thoughts and forces me to remember all those times he robbed me of all the air and words in his car. And then he cheated on me. And then, the most powerful word that I've kept in the dark uncovers the truth that I have tried so hard to bury: "No."

My mouth spits out the word as I gulp air. And I know exactly what Mrs. Skye has been talking about this whole year. The power of words. I grab his arms with both of my hands. "Fuck, no," I say.

He lets his head fall heavily onto my chest. "Whaaat?" He half-whines, breathing into my neck. "This isn't about your body again, is it?"

"I can't do this," I say.

204

He lifts up his head and I can see his eyes flicker in the dim candlelight. They are dark, thick brown, almost black. Not galaxies I realize but absences of color.

"Now, you want to talk?" he demands. "Really?"

"No, I don't want to talk," I say, calm. "I don't want to do this."

He sighs heavily. "God, you're a lot of work," he says as he pulls himself up and kneels in front of me.

"Excuse me?"

He takes my hand and massages my palm with his thumb. "I'm sorry," he says, gently. "That's not what I meant. We love each other. You want this as much as I do. And now here we are, so close to moving forward." He says this sexy and low, but I'm not the least bit turned on.

"No," I say and there are so many other words crawling up my windpipe like angry bees. My heart is pumping and the fire in my belly is churning, ready to unleash them. Give them the power of the gods.

"But you already said yes," he says, his words a whisper, a manipulative edge in them, and he slowly moves his weight back on top of me, his hand curling around my back like a vice.

My words get stuck again but not like before. This time, I can't breathe from the weight of him. "Adam," I say, stilling my pounding heart.

There's this little moment of fear, a millisecond where I think that there's nothing left of me. That I can't fight back. That I can't say what I want to say. That I can't give my words power.

And then I think *fuck that.* I think I channel Leah somehow and Mrs. Skye and Mollie and hell even Melody as I push him off of me, hard, and they all open my mouth for me but it's me who says it, and it feels so good, "Fuck off!" I push him as hard as I can, my arms becoming as strong as my convictions.

And just like that, Adam's body melts away from me; I can breathe so fully that I think I must be sucking up all of his air too.

I sit up and hug my knees, breathing in and out, feeling lots of different things: there's some shame and embarrassment and there's a familiar lump in my throat. But, I breathe. And steady myself. And think *now what?* I would give anything to talk to Leah because I know she'd tell me what else to say. I mean, what's the next thing you say after telling someone to fuck off? But for now, it's just me. Alone in Adam's dark room that smells like pine from a candle he forgot to blow out.

When I look up, Adam's standing by the door.

"You got something to say?" he demands. He sounds more hurt than angry.

"Like what?" I ask, dumbfounded. Does he expect me to apologize?

"You come here, you lead me on, and then you act like this. That's some psychopathic bullshit."

I'm not sure why, but I choose this moment to start laughing. It's the complete opposite of what I expect from myself, but I can't help it. "Nothing's wrong with me," I say and pause. "I think, actually, there's something wrong with *you*."

"Wow, you're just like *them*," he says, and I'm not entirely sure who he means. "Just like my mom. Fucking bitches. You all are."

I stand up in the semi-darkness feeling lightheaded and watch his body leave the room; I can hear him mumbling that word *bitch* over and over.

When I hear him banging around in the kitchen, I creep quietly downstairs, heave open that deceptive, oak door, and slide into my car, turning my music up loud.

Before I drive off, I take a quick look in the rearview mirror. There are no tears in my eyes. They are refusing to fall. The quote from Leah's painting blares in my mind, louder than the radio: *Nothing I accept about myself...*

Bitch? I wonder, staring at my reflection. I let the word roll casually off my tongue a few times, just to test it out.

And I know that Hillary Clinton and even Mrs. Skye and certainly Leah would agree with me: that the word, if used in the right moment, is one bad ass compliment.

*   *   *   *

I stay in on Saturday night. Not that I have anywhere to go. Or anyone to be with. I am completely alone. *Alone. Alone. Alone.*

This is what I've been avoiding for months, this cruel reality that I don't belong. The good news is that I do not feel regret when I think of Adam; if anything, I feel relief. Now that it's over, I feel like I can finally begin to piece myself back together, and I know where I need to start.

Because what I keep coming back to, over and over, is Leah.

Upstairs in my room, I go through old photographs of us, hoping to find something that I can hold on to. There's the one of us from the second grade Halloween party: Leah is a cat with black tights and leotard. Her hands are behind her back and she's leaning forward a bit, a giant smile on her face. I'm a witch with silver, tinsel hair and an oversized, shapeless, black dress. My smile is so big that it makes my eyes squinty. There's another one of us in a store in Cape Cod. We both donned giant, round brimmed hats, like the ones women wear at the Kentucky Derby. Leah had fallen back into my arms pretending to pass out from the heat--a trust fall--and I had caught her while my mom snapped a picture. You can't see her face because of the hat, but my mouth's wide open, feigning shock.

Then there's the one of us from our birthday party with matching outfits. This is when I saw how different we really were, when I started comparing our sizes. Or am I just seeing this now? Because when I really think about it, I remember how happy I felt then. With Leah, despite my jealousy, I belonged.

I put away the pictures and take out my mother's poem and reread it for the hundredth time. I want to ask her about it, but I know she'll just wave it off like it's nothing and then change the subject. The more I think about it, about her, about how so many of her words have made me reject my own body, the more my own words get trapped inside of me.

So, even though it's late and cold, even for a March night, I put on a sports bra, warm pants, and a sweatshirt. I find my headphones and sneakers buried underneath some clothes in my closet. I think that this might help me clear my head or at least rattle my thoughts enough to get them out onto paper, and, for the first time, I don't care how many calories I burn.

When my feet hit the pavement, I'm so thankful that my body remembers that it actually loves to run.

*   *   *   *

On Monday morning, I ask Dad for a ride to school.

"Adam's not driving you anymore?" Dad asks.

"It's over," I say simply and put on my backpack, wait for his sarcastic response.

But he's silent instead, just nodding his head. "Okay, do you want me to make you breakfast?" he asks eventually, "I can go in a little late."

"No thanks. Can we leave now actually? I have to do something before first period."

Dad's already warmed up the car and I'm thankful since it's cold and damp out. I expect a quiet, peaceful ride but instead, when he slides in the seat, he asks me, "So are you and your mother fighting?"

I think I'd prefer sarcasm over this question. "No, not really." I push the button on the window and watch it roll down. The cold air hits my face and so I roll it back up. "Why?"

He starts the engine and backs out with his arm almost around me. "No reason, just haven't seen you guys talking much lately. You both are always talking so much that I can't get a word in."

I roll my eyes at him even though he's looking at the road. "Dad, you *barely* talk to *us*. I think you could go an entire week without saying a word."

"Okay, that might be true. But you and your mom? You talk nonstop. There's a lot of silence at our house lately and it's making me uncomfortable."

"I don't feel like talking to her lately, Dad. I mean, I know she loves me, but sometimes she says things that make me feel shitty. It's like she wants me to feel bad about how I look so that I'll change. It's like she doesn't accept me just how I am." My voice is breaking, so I push the button to roll down the window again. *Down.* I catch my breath. *Up.*

Dad's nodding his head slowly and then he rubs his scruff, thinking. "Hmmmm." He's quiet for the rest of the short ride. I think that must be the end of the conversation and wonder why I even answered him honestly.

When we get to my school though, he parks and turns to me. "I know it's really hard to see this because you're so young. But I think your mother associates good looks with being happy. You're mother is beautiful, and she's afraid. For some reason, she thinks that's all she is, and, I think, believes that if she loses it, things will fall apart, like she'll lose everything that she's fought hard to get. It doesn't make sense, right? But does that make sense?"

It's the most I've heard him say, like, ever, so I shake my head no and continue playing with the window, pouting a little like a child, hoping that he'll continue. I'm quiet trying to soak in all of his words so that I remember them.

"Unfortunately," he continues, "I guess she wants the same for you but she doesn't recognize that all of the other things about you--like how you're smart and sensitive and creative--are actually more important. And I'm sorry for that. But she loves you. And you'll have to be the one to figure out what's really behind the picture of her that you don't see."

"Ya, that makes sense, I guess," I say.

Dad takes a deep breath. "Okay, now get out. I'm exhausted. I'm pretty sure I've made my talking quota for the whole month."

"Ya, I'd say you're good. See ya, Dad."

         *   *   *   *

I head into school trying not to think about Mom. I really do get what Dad was saying; I just am not ready to process it right now. Besides, I have something else I have to do. Dad has confirmed something I've been thinking about all night. About what's behind the picture.

When I walk into school, I find Leah's painting and

stand inches away from it, squinting my eyes, urging myself to see what's beyond it. There are things becoming unstuck in my mind and I'm hoping that this face to face will help me finally sort them all out.

I'm not sure how long I stand there with the halls empty and my thoughts swirling, but, at some point, students fill the corridor, and I feel a gentle tap on my shoulder. "Hey," someone whispers.

It's Melody.

"Hey," I say. I haven't talked to her since my fight with Leah, and I still feel a little jealous that she has my best friend all to herself, but I'm not so angry about it. If anything, Melody is a piece to figuring out Leah's puzzle.

"She's so talented, right?" she says, her eyes on the painting, shaking her head in disbelief. She moves closer to it, like she's going to touch it but stops, puts both of her hands in her back pockets. I look closely at Melody, inspecting her like I did the painting. There's something going on here that I can't name. Some proof of her innocence that's just beginning to materialize.

"Who is it?" I ask, more hurt than anything else that I have to ask Melody this. So hurt that I don't know the answer, and angry at myself for being the cause. "Who is the girl in the painting?"

"Wow," Melody says, surprised. "Can't you tell?" She looks from me to the painting, smiling mysteriously. "It's a secret," she says, putting her finger to her lips. "I'm not supposed to tell."

I try to smile back at her. "Can you tell Leah that I love it?"

"Why don't you tell her yourself?" Melody asks.

"I don't think she wants to talk to me right now. I've tried."

"Try again."

The warning bell rings but Melody sits down next to me. We're quiet, watching as students pass us on the way to wherever they're going. When the halls are nearly empty, Melody stands. "We should get going."

"Okay," I tell her, but I don't stand up.

"Hey Aster," she says, real quiet. "I meant what I said, about telling Leah. I know things are complicated right now between you two, but I think she needs you. You know she'd never admit it, but I know she misses you."

"Ya, okay. Maybe."

"You coming?" she asks.

"In a minute," I say. But I'm not going to first period. Instead, I sit across from the painting, my back against the wall. I take out my notebook and, finally, I write.

I *wonder if you were alone*
when your paintbrush made its first mark.
Did you know
that the ribbon
would wind itself tightly like a noose
binding her mouth into
a suffocating silence?
with a delicate twirl
of your wand
her facial features shut off
from the blunt end of my apologies

Is it you?
I can't be sure

I wonder if it hurt
when you finally took the brush away
did the final image
hold you accountable for the loss
of your own voice
did you try to erase the patterns
so I could not recognize
the finishing touches

I thought it was you
but now I'm not sure
our friendship a tightrope of uncertainty

I wonder if you lost yourself
beneath those orange hues
of an artist's sacrifice
while your hands blistered
all I had to offer you was silence

a gift of utter betrayal

And in the battered disarray of a magician's touch
is that when you found her?

Is that the moment you fell in love?

19

It's easy to make connections when your heart becomes free of some of its selfishness and shame and you allow it to heal through poetry and art. When you commit to being alone with your thoughts because maybe it's easier than trying to mold yourself like clay, you see things a lot more clearly.

After school, when I finally pull into Leah's driveway, it's pouring out. I pull my sweatshirt hood over my head and sprint to her door.

I enter her house without knocking which would be a normal thing for me to do a few months ago. Plus, I know her mom isn't home, like usual. But as I stand on the tiled landing, I feel like an intruder. *What am I even going to say?* "Leah?" I whisper, but there's no way she can hear me above the pounding rain.

Downstairs, the TV blares but no one's watching. "Leah?" Silence.

I feel terrified all of the sudden. She might possibly hate me, but I can't go before I at least explain and apologize. "Leah," I yell more loudly.

"Yo," she calls. I can hear her coming down the stairs, and then she steps into the kitchen in her Kids Town work shirt. "Hey," she says slowly. "Did you call me?" She looks down at her phone.

"No, I figured you wouldn't answer."

"Probably not," she says. Smart ass. "What are you doing here?" she demands but she doesn't sound mad, just curious. "I'm leaving for work in a few minutes."

I decide not to hold back. "I saw your painting," I start. "Actually, I saw it awhile ago and I've been staring at it almost every day. And it got me thinking. Is it Melody?"

If the question suprises her, she doesn't let on. "What are you talking about?" She opens the fridge, rummages through it, ignoring me. "You want something?" she asks.

"Is it Melody?" I ask again. "In the picture? Leah, it's cool, you know? I think I get it. Are you in love with her?"

She closes the fridge door and sighs heavily. "It's really none of your fucking business," she says and sits down on one of the bar stools, opens up a can of Coke. I sit on the other one even though she doesn't invite me to.

"I'm sorry," I say. "You're right. It's not my business."

"You're soaked," Leah responds, distracted. I look down. I had forgotten about the rain. My shirt sticks to me and my hair drips on the linoleum.

"It's raining."

Leah puts both of her hands on her temples, rubs them slowly. "It's been a weird year," she says to me, an explanation for all of those lost hours.

"It's okay," I stumble through my words, feeling farther from Leah than I knew possible. "I'm sorry. I'll go. I just wanted to tell you that I miss you. And that I'm sorry for being so pathetic about Melody. And that if you guys are together, which I know is none of my business, but that I understand. I don't know why it's such a secret, but I'll keep it for both of you. I know I was a shitty friend, but you can trust me."

Leah doesn't respond, just continues to massage her temples. I'm about to leave when suddenly she says, "Why didn't you say anything?"

"What?" I say, fishing in my purse for my keys.

"To Max. You let me stand there alone. You didn't defend me or anything."

I sit back down, take a deep breath. "I thought you

could handle yourself. I didn't know you needed me. I'm so sorry. I should have been there for you." She nods slowly. I look down at my hands and inspect my knuckles. "I guess I also thought that, if I said something to him, he'd turn on me next."

I wait, but she doesn't say anything else. She stands up suddenly. "Aster, I really I have to go to work."

"Okay," I say but I keep going. "I was scared of him, of Max, of what he could say to me to tear me down. But me? I'm scared of everyone and everything. But you're never scared. What is it with Max?"

"I don't know, it's just I can't explain," she says, tripping over her words. She looks at her phone again. "I'm going to be late."

We exchange an awkward goodbye and she leaves first. I'm not sure whether or not she forgives me, but I'm certain that I'm right about Melody because Leah always tells the truth, and when she can't, she flees.

* * * *

It's the same thing that happened when I found out she was gay during an innocent game of truth or dare in junior high at a sleepover. When Leah finally chose truth, one girl asked her to reveal the name of her crush, and Leah burst out laughing and ran out of the room. Later, when I finally ran after her and found her outside on our friend's porch, she looked horrified. "I can't answer that question," she told me.

"Oh my God. Who is it?" I asked. I was worried it was Peter Sevelt who always helped Leah with her math homework but who also apparently told every boy on his football team that he saw her tits one day when she leaned too far over to pick up a pencil he had knocked off the desk for that exact reason.

"I can't tell you," she said and clamped her mouth shut with her hands. But then she took her hands away for a second. "It's a girl," she said quickly.

"So it's not Peter then?" I asked, relieved.

"Star did you hear what I said?" she asked, sounding impatient. "I mean, I think I'm gay. Don't you care? Doesn't that bother you?"

"No, why would it?" I answered honestly. "I mean, as long as I don't have to be gay too then I think we're good," I joked. "Because I'm like really in love with Justin Hall and I don't want that feeling to go away." Justin was my crush at that moment because he wrote his own song lyrics and read every book assigned in our English class.

"Ya, I think you're good," Leah laughed.

"You're a terrible liar," I told her.

"My only flaw," she said. "Just don't tell anyone, okay?"

"It's not my business to tell."

I think everyone always assumed Leah was just too good for the boys at our school, so no one ever asked her again to name her crush, saving her from ever having to admit the truth.

*   *   *   *

I don't hear from Leah until the following Friday night when she texts me and asks to meet her for coffee the next morning. I'm so surprised and happy that I have to contain myself from responding with all exclamation points.

I arrive at the coffee shop early so that I can sort through my feelings. Although I'm happy that Leah's speaking to me again, I'm not sure she missed me at all.

I get a coffee and take a seat near an open window. Minutes later, I see Leah enter through the front door and following behind her, not surprisingly, is Melody.

When they come over, Melody seems to be back to her old self. She hugs me; it's a longer than necessary hug as usual but I try not to pull away. Leah holds two coffees in her hand and puts them on the table. We small talk for a bit; first about the torrential downpours from yesterday, and then today's sun appearing in the sky, acting as if nothing happened, making the roads glisten. Proof that Spring is actually here.

"So?" I finally say, giving them both a full one second look.

Melody looks at Leah and nods. "We've been together for a while," she explains. "Since last summer actually."

I know this is what Leah came here to tell me, and I want to be happy for them. But I still feel so left out of her life.

Leah must see the disappointment on my face. "I'm so sorry I didn't tell you, Star. It's just that Melody wasn't...well she still really isn't...ready to tell people that..." her voice trails off. It is so not like her. It must be love.

"I'm into girls," Melody says, tapping her fingers on the table, finishing Leah's thought. Leah tilts her head, smirking. It's probably the first time she's heard Melody say this. "And I'm scared. I'm not ready for the whole world to know. But, I'm trying. Now you know." She pauses, takes a sip of her coffee. "And Levi knows of course."

Levi. I look down at my hands. There are so many things I want to ask, but this isn't about me.

"I'm glad you told me," I say to them. "And obviously I'm happy for you." I say it. It's just hard to feel it fully, but maybe, hopefully, I will in time. "And Max?" I ask Leah, suddenly remembering the real reason we haven't spoken. "Did he know?"

Leah hesitates. "Ya, he knew about us. We weren't always so secret. During the summer once. We thought we were alone…" Her voice trails off.

"He never said anything to us," Melody picks up the story for her. "But the look on his face when he realized who we were and that we were together…it spooked us both. We didn't think anything of it until he started harassing her in gym class. Leah wanted to tell him off, but I begged her not to. I thought if she did then he'd ruin us. Well, he'd ruin me. I never thought he'd treat Leah like he did." She looks down, averting my eyes.

My face burns, ashamed of what I let happen. "Leah, I'm so sorry. I should have done something. I should have--"

It all makes sense now. How Leah *did* hear everything but chose to swallow her words in order to protect her new relationship. How her silence only fueled Max's anger until he found the words that would hurt her most.

"I know," Leah says softly. "I get it, I do. He had too much control over me and the whole situation. And then when he said that--about me not living in this country--he knew the one thing he could say to, well, diminish me."

"It was my fault," Melody says. "I should never have asked you to stay quiet."

But Melody's silence must have pained her more. That's why Leah painted ribbons that silenced and hid her. And I wonder if it even *is* Melody in that painting. Or does the image represent all of us who are forced into silence or hiding when it comes to society's rejections?

"It's over with," Leah says ands smiles at Melody. The comfort between them still feels like a slap; is it my fault that I missed it all? "There's no changing someone like Max. There's nothing I could have said."

"I know but I also made you lie to your best friend. That was unfair. Star," she says, facing me and staring at me intently. "I'm so so sorry. This-" she motions to me and Leah, "this is my fault."

I smile at her sincerity. There really is so much more to her than I was willing to see.

"You wanna hug it out?" she asks, peeking up, smiling shyly.

I laugh and Leah rolls her eyes. "I know she's *very* affectionate. It takes some getting used to."

It's almost noon when I check my phone. Before I leave, Melody hugs me again, pressing every inch of herself into my body. Mid-hug, she whispers in my ear, "Levi still asks about you." She must feel me pull away, so she slides her hands to my arms to make me stay.

"I just...I thought *you* were into him. I thought..."

Melody stifles a laugh. "I'm sorry, Aster. He's like a brother."

"I know *now* you're not," I say, gesturing towards Leah, and I don't want to talk about it but the words come out anyways. "It's just that I saw you two in the halls at school. You looked so...comfortable, and he looked at you with such...I don't know...I thought it was love?" I feel stupid saying it now. I couldn't even see his face.

"Levi has always taken care of me. I was doing stupid shit and he was trying to help. That's what he does. He knew about Leah, about my drinking which was so stupid. I was just so lost...but, honestly, he looks at me the same way that Leah looks at you. Ya, it's love, because we are best friends."

I look over at Leah who loves me, who has been my voice for so many years, who smiles at me now. And no matter how many times we get lost, I hope I always know how to get back to her. But maybe that's why it's time to stop using her voice and step fully into my own.

Before Leah leaves, she says, "I just don't understand why you went back to that snake."

"I know, I know," I put my hands up defensively. "But that's over. We're officially done."

Leah raises her eyebrows. "Really?"

"Ya, he doesn't deserve me." I'm not sure if I believe it, but I try out the idea.

Leah smiles. "Can we talk about it later?"

"Of course. Come by tomorrow."

To see Leah and Melody

completely comfortable in each other's presence
makes me grip
the steering wheel hard
makes me want to drift off course

To watch Leah
look so comfortable
and finally in love
makes me, the interloper,
pull over,
roll down the window,
and taste the rain
that remains in the air

And Melody looking so vulnerable
her hands finally to herself
her smile completely sincere
makes me shut my eyes
and remember that time I saw
her and Levi,
in what I interpreted as lust.

What other parts of my life
have I gotten utterly wrong?

20

"There's a part of me that still doesn't understand you," Leah begins when she finally comes over to talk, sitting on my bed like we never spent a minute apart.

"I should explain," I say, but then I'm quiet.

I have dreaded this conversation that I would have with you one day, and I should have forced myself to speak so long ago, and maybe then the shame that I felt would not have burrowed itself so far inside of me and become a part of my truths. But shame loves secrets; it feeds off its silence, grows fast and invisible like bacteria.

Where do I start? How do I begin to tell you the story of how I became obsessed with perfection, how I wrapped my hopes in something non-existent, how you were my best friend but also caused so much of the pain I felt, even if unintentionally?

"Yes, please explain," Leah says. "You have this perfect life." She finally sits down and faces me. "I've actually resented you for it at times."

You lived with shame too. How didn't I ever see it? While I longed for thinness and a flawless image, you wanted a different part of my life. We talked about everything except the parts of ourselves that troubled us, even though the explanation of our self-hatred would have eased our pain.

I became blinded by my jealousy. It warped my vision of you, of who you were, of what you really needed from me.

"You were my first friend when I moved here, and my only friend for a while. I relied on you to make me feel like I belonged. *You* always belonged even if you didn't feel it. Do you know what I mean? And so when Max said those things to me, and you didn't say anything...I don't know, I just thought how I didn't belong at all. Not with you, not here, not anywhere. It made me feel completely alone."

I know exactly what you mean. But neither one of us belongs. Maybe that's what binds us together. We both have had those same ribbons tied around our mouths, cutting off the oxygen to our voices. We both have battled a silence. What I most regret is that I failed to do what poetry taught me: I focused on the differences between us instead of what connects us. And in those spaces that I left wide open, we fell away from each other.

"Leah looks at me and wipes her eyes. "Say something," she says.

You don't want any more apologies. You want an explanation of who I am...the way I see myself that made me voiceless. There's no accurate synonym for shame. And there's no easy way to describe it.

"I wanted *your* life," I say, lamely. *"This.* I've hated myself, my body, for a really long time. I hated you for *looking* perfect. It's just nothing I could talk about because I was always too ashamed. And now I just feel like a terrible friend."

There are so many things I never told you, never told anyone. About the crash diets, the binging and purging, the 5 am runs followed by the 5 pm workouts, the obsession with counting calories, the fact that every single minute of my life, I'm thinking about my weight. I've kept it all from you. I've kept it all from my narrative too. The truth has barely even made its way into my poetry. I was completely alone in it, isolating and protecting the shame that manifested, believing that this self-hatred might protect me, might impel me to reconstruct my body: a complicated formula for improvement.

"I know it sounds so stupid now, but you eat literally anything you want, and you're still so skinny. I eat non-stop healthy vegetables and I'm twice your size."

"Okay, you are *not* twice my size, you lunatic. And you're just super healthy. I always think, *wow I wish I could eat like her."*

Eat like me? So spend every second counting calories, feeling guilty over eating white toast, each day consumed by how I will burn off any extra calories?

"But you could," I say.

"But those aren't my habits. I've been home alone since I was a kid. I ate whatever snack was in the cabinet. Your mom makes healthy meals and doesn't allow junk in your house. We live in two totally different worlds."

"That's fair," I say, "It's just annoying as *fuck.* Like, why do I still look like this?"

"That's what I don't get. When I look at you, I just see you as perfect. You're an athlete, you know. Are you super skinny? No. But you got these crazy, strong legs and bad ass arms. And you always look put together. You get good grades, you're smart as hell, and you never lose your cool like I do. You always look like you got your shit together. It's just, I don't know, better than pretty."

"Really?" I shake my head, unable to see this picture of myself. "But, I just want to look like..I don't know...one of *them."* I gesture at all of the women on my mirror. "That's who I should be."

I'm realizing how ridiculous my wants are...how many things in life I have but don't ever give those things a second thought. How I am all of these other things besides my body.

Leah looks the pictures over with a pompous confidence. "Nah, you don't look like any of them. You've got your own thing going, and you don't need to pose like a pouty little girl to get what you want. Are you really just here to please everyone else? And like I said before, *no one* actually looks like that. It's all an illusion. You're fucking real."

"Ya, I am." I sigh. "And I'll always have rolls, and my thighs will always chafe."

"Don't they have spandex for that?" she asks and I laugh. "Why do you always think you have to change yourself?" She stops herself. "Ya, actually, I get it. I guess I tried to change this year too. Max really dug low. I've never felt so ashamed of my own skin."

"Which is completely ridiculous," I say.

"I see that now," she says, "same with you."

"I just wish I could see myself through your eyes."

I've only ever seen myself through my mother's eyes, or the eyes of those who saw me as unworthy.

"We should tear these pictures down," Leah suggests. "I'm pretty sure they're giving me nightmares."

"Ya, you're probably right," I answer but neither one of us move. We just stare and I wonder, *what would happen if I shifted the focus?*

I shift the focus by giving someone else the pen

Loving yourself was always the problem
no matter what, there was nothing I could say
to make you see
no matter how many times you suffered in darkness
your refusal of lights--
you continued to nudge me away
reeling your body towards distant corners
so that you could further concede to a lie
that was told to you your whole life
about your imperfections
and then told, insidiously,
that you were to blame.

This damage has rendered, not hostility,
towards an unforgiving world
but guilt in your own heart
for not measuring up to a standard

Yet, when I look at you
I see that, yes, your body
is maybe imperfect
but it's also strong enough
to shatter glass
and defy fairy tales
and tell your own story

When I look at you
I see that you are worthy of love

When will the mirror reflect
to you what I see?

{ SPRING }

21

Sometimes, Mrs. Skye leaves her classroom door open for students who feel inspired and want to continue writing during lunch. Today, I sneak in her room with my sad bag of loose fruits and protein. I close the door and take a seat in the back of the room with my laptop and am sorting through some writing when the door opens again and Mollie pokes her head in. "Hey," she says. "I thought I saw you walk in here."

I'm happy to see her. She has that effect on people.

"You wanna eat with me?" I ask, holding up my apple.

She smiles and nods her head. "I already ate, but I

can eat again."

"You can share mine," I say, holding up my lunch bag. "Can I ask you something?" I say after she sits beside me and goes through the rest of my food in my lunch bag. She pulls out each piece, inspecting it closely.

"Anything," she says, holding up a small container I've filled with hummus. "But can I try this?"

I slide over the raw veggies. "For dipping."

She chews uncertainly. "These are gross," she says, but continues eating them. "Ask away."

"Don't take this the wrong way because I think you're great." I pause, unsure of how to phrase the question. "But how come you like yourself so much?"

Mollie reacts with a small shrug, like she's been asked this same question a hundred times. "It's kind of a funny story." She takes her time finishing her celery. "And a little tragic."

I wait patiently, unsure that we're close enough friends for her to tell me. "It's okay. You don't have to tell me."

"Oh no, it's fine actually. I've told this story so many times. My therapist thinks that the more I tell it to people I trust, the more distant the experience will become, so eventually it will be like I'm telling someone else's story. Like a character in a book, you know? Instead of, like, me."

"Therapist?" I ask.

"Ya, I've been seeing her for a while. Loving yourself takes daily practice and *loads* of fucking therapy." She smiles and takes a big bite of one of my carrots.

"Got it. So what's your story?"

"Well," she says swallowing. "I was an extremely shy child and really just wanted to stay in my room most of the day and draw. I didn't have many friends, and my parents thought I was depressed. Anyways, in seventh grade, they signed me up for this club at my church with other kids my age that struggled with social situations. We had to sit around *all* day and like *interact* with adults watching and criticizing us. It was God *awful.*"

"Sounds like the opposite of spiritual."

"Yup. I dreaded going and hated my parents for it, even though they were just trying to help. And I fought them every single Saturday--that's when the club met--but then, I met a boy."

I raise my eyebrows. "A boy?"

"Ya, but don't get that starry look in your eyes."

She frowns. "So, this boy and I started flirting and hanging out, sitting next to each other during meetings. The good thing about the club--or cult, or whatever--was that they'd eventually give us time to be alone and they'd organize events for us, these pathetic kids who could barely make eye contact and some of us stuttered and some of us had panic attacks and most of us cut ourselves at one time or another." She slides up her sleeve, revealing a small scar.

"Mollie!" I say, stunned. Of course I've heard stories of kids cutting, but I would never think Mollie would do something like that to herself.

"It's okay. Really. I'm okay now."

"So what happened with this boy?"

"Well, one day we decided to skip the club and go to his house since his parents were never around, busy doing church-goer goody goody shit, I guess." I think I know where this is going, and I want to stop her words. "I was so innocent. He was two years older and I thought he just wanted to play video games but, well, he wanted to do other things too." Her voice is shaky now. She takes a deep breath. "He wanted to…." Her voice trails off. "This is the part that I have trouble saying."

"Oh God. Did he make you?" I ask, thinking about Adam and shuddering at our last experience, how close we'd come even though I didn't want to.

She shakes her head. "No, but he tried although he didn't get too far. His mom came home early…she came right in his room and I was in there. He had already gotten me to take my shirt off."

"Oh, Mollie, no," I say and put my hand over my mouth.

"I ran out of there as fast as I could. Luckily, his mom didn't know who I was because she never called my parents. I couldn't tell my parents at first, I was so ashamed, and so they forced me to go back to the club, unable to understand my change of emotions. I begged them not to. But I was young and I always did what my parents told me, no matter what. So I showed up at the meeting. He had already told everyone that we hooked up The friends that I thought I made, those same kids who had scars like me, one of them wrote *slut* on a piece of paper and scribbled my name underneath. They passed it around in our sacred circle until it got to me."

"Shit. I'm so sorry."

"Thanks," she says and picks up another carrot. "I stayed through the whole meeting that day, feeling dirty and ashamed. But I'm lucky. When my mom picked me up, I burst into tears and she made me tell her everything. And I did tell her everything. I didn't realize what a kick ass mom I had until that moment. She completely took my side, got me out of that club, and found me a really good therapist."

"What happened to the boy?"

"My mom called his mom and there was a lot of denial on the other end. There wasn't much we could do about it. It was my word against his. Thankfully, I didn't see him again. Well, not until this year."

"You saw him?"

"Well, ya, because he goes to this school. I've passed him in the halls but he pretends he doesn't know me, which is fine. I really don't think he'll bother me again. I mean, I know a lot of his secrets, like how he was before he grew out of his completely socially awkward phase, but he still freaks me out. I don't know, he has this weird power, like he's untouchable."

And I don't want to pry but I can't help my curiosity. Because this kid, if he's two years older than Mollie, he's in my grade. "What's his name?" I ask.

She pauses. "His name..."

But I think I already know.

"His name is Max."

*   *   *   *

Friday night, half of Mrs. Skye's class meets at the

school to go to a slam poetry event in the city.

The bus is late, so we all stand outside shivering, talking in little groups, our breath visible in the night air. I stand with Mollie.

"I don't mean to bring Max up again," I say to her quietly, "but a friend of mine had some issues with him this year."

"Really?"

"Ya, you know Leah? Well, he basically told her to go back to her own country."

"Asshole," Mollie says.

"I know. I mean Leah *is* from this country. And even if she wasn't, it still would have been messed up. Max is so high on Trump it's scary."

"He's pathetic."

Mrs. Skye comes over to tell us the bus will be here shortly. She then asks me how the revisions on my poem are going.

"You're still going to let me revise?" I ask. "That was, like, months ago."

"Well, ya, as long as it's worth my time. Some poems need tending to, like a garden. And sometimes it takes a while to get the flowers to grow. I'll be here for the rest of the year." She winks at me.

I haven't thought about that poem for some time, the one about my mother. I don't know why it's so hard to write about her, like I'm betraying her with every word I put on the page. I'm still avoiding her as well. I have learned that if I just engage with her in simple conversations, like small talk, then there's less of a chance that she'll say something hurtful. I have also stayed out of her bedroom and have kept her out of mine thinking that the more enclosed setting with only one escape might give her more of an opportunity to unleash a negative comment or two.

The bus ends up being a half hour late so when we get to the event a girl is already on the stage, performing a solo piece on gender and sexuality. She references her vagina so many times and even though her descriptions are cloaked in euphemism, Mrs. Skye's face turns red.

She's sitting between me and Mollie and she swears it's because she likes being lined up with center stage but I know it's because we can't shut our mouths when we're together.

The small theater smells like sweat and spoken words ricochet off the walls. The audience is loud, like they are part of the show. They snap their fingers to show praise for the emotions that resonate with them. They yell and whoop at the strongest words and phrases. I don't know if it's because the air conditioning is broken or there's just too many bodies in a little space, but it feels like the peak of summer in here.

"I can't breathe," Mollie says, fanning the program in front of us. "And it smells like my brother's gym bag."

"Shhh!" Mrs. Skye whispers and gestures at the stage.

The group slams woo the crowd and steal the show but the one act that leaves me speechless is delivered by a large, Black girl. When she walks up to the microphone and lifts her head to speak into the respected silence, her hips take up so much space on that stage. There's a part of my conscious, the one that society has molded, that maybe whispers an ugly truth about her weight, yet a louder part of me settles into my seat thinking about this girl's *presence.* She's not just taking up space; instead she pulsates with an energy that earns respect for every inch that she moves in. Her confidence stares me in the eyes like a dare.

When she begins, her quiet voice tells the story of a girl kept down by insults. How she never felt safe from critics who saw her sinful hips as incorrect proportions and her monstrous legs as losses. Towards the end, her voice gets louder and surer of itself as she rallies against the voices that chained her. Then she ends with the message that even when her thoughts conspired against her, her strong body, the body she chose to respect despite the body-shaming, showed up to face the battles. The last line of her poem describes her body in one word: *blessing.*

It's the last word I expect to hear, and as the crowd stands to cheer, the word reverberates with my own heartbeat. Mollie looks over at me, still clapping.

"Are you crying?" she yells above the noise.

I wipe my face and laugh. "Fuck that was good." If it was any other day, I don't think her words would have moved me in such a powerful way. But, tonight, her poem is medicine.

Mrs. Skye elbows me. "Don't say fuck." Her eyes go wide and she places her hand quickly over her mouth to erase the word. Then she laughs. "But you're right. That was fucking amazing."

Mollie and I laugh so hard that Mrs. Skye threatens to sit between us on the bus ride home. We zip it up.

Blessing.

On the ride home
the word is still
alive in the air

I close my eyes and catch it
with glue hands

letting the B bind itself to my clavicle
while the L presses itself to that space
between my breasts
and the ESS drip down slowly
stick to my belly
like honey

the ING spreads across my lower belly
like hands that speak for themselves

I settle into this body *blessed*
by this one word of worthiness

Is a blessing the opposite of shame?

Is it a blessing to realize
that you have the right to love something
that you were taught to hate?

22

After the poetry slam, I'm inspired. I know I'm ready to revise my poem for Mrs. Skye and maybe it's not about my mother anymore; it's about all of us who experience the trouble with pretty.

I think about those pictures on my mirror that I taped there for motivation. Are there other girls who use this same mode of punishment? Are there others who look at these flawless women and find unhealthy ways to get to this point B?

I think about the advertisements that Mrs. Skye had us collect, and I know that it's simply a marketing tactic that's used to sell products, but those repeated images still wreak havoc on all of us who are still learning who we should be. Mrs. Skye said that the body type we see in the media is only two percent of the population, and that girls cannot diet their way into this size two figure. We still fight hard for thinness, flat abs, and a thigh gap, but, more often than not, genetics will win.

I think about the young girl I saw one time at a Red Sox game while I was in the bathroom and she couldn't have been older than ten, but she was just staring at herself in the mirror, changing her facial expression and her clothes. Smiling, frowning, kissy face; shirt off the shoulder, shirt on the shoulder. Turning around to look at her back side, another kissy face. Outside, Big Papi was probably gearing up to hit another homerun, but this girl had only pretty on her mind.

I think about the election, the focus on Hillary Clinton's body and aged face. Is that happens when a woman tries to be something other than pretty?

I think about my mother's preoccupation with thinness even though she's smart and successful. Will she ever see her other strengths or will this always be her priority?

"Aster, come here," Mom calls to me while I'm trying my hardest to get all of my ideas down on paper. Even though I'm thinking clearly, I still don't want to disappoint Mrs. Skye with mediocre revisions.

"What's up?" I yell from my room, not yet willing to step inside that door and possibly stop any progress that I've made.

"Come in here," she yells back, "I have something for you!"

Knowing that I can't avoid her forever and mildly curious about what she has for me, I walk into her bedroom. Even though it's a weekend afternoon,

Mom has on a white and blue striped button down shirt with leggings; her hair is curled and rests neatly on her shoulders.

"Hi!" She's all smiles as she gestures towards her bed. There are two light-colored Spring dresses displayed there with matching blue flats. My first thought, *What if they don't fit? She definitely bought them a size too small.*

"What are these for?" I ask.

"Oh you know, just because." She sits on the edge of the bed and runs her fingers over one of the dresses. "Dad told me that you and Adam broke up again. I just thought--"

"Oh, so what are you and Dad *married* now," I say, cutting her off, unable to hold back my anger and also wanting to deflect any comment she might say about making me pretty.

"Aster, we *are* married. What's that supposed to mean?"

"Forget it," I say, waving her off. "Adam and I broke up over a month ago. I'm fine."

Mom puts her hands in her lap. "Why didn't you tell me?" she asks, and her voice is quiet. "You usually tell me everything."

"Well, let's see. The last time I told you, when my

heart was completely *broken,* you called me fat and said I needed to lose weight."

"What? I would *never* call you *fat,*" she says, putting her hand over her chest like she's pledging allegiance.

"Well, you didn't have to say that *word.* You've said it a thousand times without actually saying it."

"I would *never* call you fat," she repeats.

I give her time to elaborate, or apologize, but she just sits there, looking up at me. I've never seen her look so sad. Mom's always high energy with a smile on her face even if she's stressed or tired or aggravated with Dad. When she's not working, she's working out or cooking or cleaning or making plans. She never stops long enough to feel any sort of negative emotion but survives on endorphins and caffeine. Seeing her still like this, her sadness visible, almost paralyzes me.

This sadness, this dissatisfaction, this stillness, I know is what's really behind the picture of her, and I hate that I want to apologize. I've forever been the complacent daughter, wanting to please everyone, especially my mother.

It's just that I never wanted her to be sad. I saw what Luke's absence did to her, how often she would tell him, "I miss you" or "Come home for dinner," and how he would never reciprocate. How he fled from our lives before he even left home, and Mom just kept moving, moving, going, running, working so she did not have to confront the truth that she had no connection with her first child. And then, in time, she and Dad grew apart for no good reason. Maybe it was her fault with her long hours and obsessive health routines, but he didn't fight to salvage it either; he settled for their mundane marriage where he could speak little and have his own space. And my mom, from what my young eyes could see, was lonely; maybe no one else saw it, but I did, and I wanted to please her in every possible way I could.

I sit down beside her, let my head drop into my hands, and breathe. "Thank you for the clothes," I finally manage.

She picks up one of the dresses, shakes it like she's trying to shake out sand, and folds it. "We can take them back if they don't fit. Or if you don't like them," she says quickly.

"No, I love them. Thank you." I ask. Because what else is there to say? I don't want her advice. I don't want the wants she has for me. I don't want these new clothes that I will wear with her dreams threaded in every seam. And it's too hard to explain who I am and what I really want because sometimes we are just strangers standing on opposites sides of pretty. But I really, *really* don't want to hurt her.

She hands me over the folded dresses and shoes,
and I hug them close to me as I leave the room
wondering and remembering the girl I was before I
worried so much about pleasing my mother, the girl
who existed before pretty came into her life.

The Trouble with Pretty
By Aster Lamonte

The trouble with pretty
is it's a dangerous imposter
spooning hope into our mouths
during meals
planting dreams of the enemy
of forever-afters
so that we believe
we will be transported
to Mount Olympus

and will the day ever arrive
when a girl is released
from its troubling hold?

So that she will remember herself
and the ocean of hope she had
before pretty came into her life
like a thief
robbing her of her far away dreams

She will go whirling and twirling
back to those times
when language built castles and forests
for her to explore
because she wanted to be a million things
besides pretty

Back then, pretty was nothing
but a muffled voice calling out in the dark
for her attention

Because there was more in her world to do
than gather this hopeless guarantee
in her hands, like sand in a sieve

23

Lately, things have been okay. Leah and I talk almost every day. She doesn't drive me to school because I think she picks up Melody, and that's okay with me. We still hang out most weekends, and sometimes I just stay in and write. Adam has left me alone, and I'm thankful for that. Sometimes I wonder if he and Liz got back together because I have seen them together. I don't feel angry or sad; I just hope that Liz gets to talk during their conversations.

On a whim, I guess because I was feeling so inspired about all of life's possibilities, I thought that I might run track again and started training. Stupidly, after my run, I did 150 sit ups in a row, tried to get up, and then fought a raging muscle spasm that landed me back on the ground, belly up.

While I'm on my back, on the floor of my gym, gasping for breath and contemplating how to get up without using any stomach muscles, a boy stands over me from behind, his crotch above my head. I can almost see up his shorts so I close my eyes. He puts his hands on his hips and peers down at me.

"You okay?" he asks and when I realize it's Levi, I

keep my eyes closed, hoping he will go away.

But, he stays. I open one eye and croak, "I'm fine." I give him the thumbs up.

He kneels down beside me. "You don't look fine."

He is painfully cute. A backwards Patriots hat (my dad would approve) and an Elton John t-shirt. He's perspiring so his hair is a little wet.

I can barely breathe. "Just a little cramp. Really, I'm fine." I can't even pick up my head from the floor, afraid of another spasm that will surely take me down again.

Levi's uncovinced. "Let me help you up at least."

I grab onto his sweaty bicep and I'm almost on my feet before another cramp sends me back to the floor. "Owwww," I stretch my hands over my head and arch my back so that my muscles stop tightening.

Levi sits, cross legged, next to me. "I'll just hang out here for a few minutes until you can actually get up. Here, have some of my water."

"Thanks," I whisper. I take his bottle and tilt it back and get a little in my mouth, but the water just mostly dribbles down my cheek and chin. I choke a little, wiping my face.

I look over at him and he all of the sudden reaches towards me and touches my cheek, wiping off a little water left there by mistake. The gesture is so intimate that I pretty much stop breathing.

"Adorable," he says, and I laugh. He takes his hand back quickly.

"You don't have to stay. Really, I'm okay."

He's looking at me, not saying a word. He inspects his shoe. "It's not a problem. I'd like to stay." He pauses, puts both arms behind him, and stretches out his mile long legs. "It's fine, really."

We stay like that for a few minutes, listening to the techno music blaring from the gym's ceiling speakers. I think about apologizing to him about what happened but how can I tell him now, in this dirty space covered with lint balls and sweaty equipment, where I can't even stand, what an absolute idiot I was.

When all of my muscles in my stomach relax, even though my insides are flipping just from looking at him, I can finally sit up and then stand. Levi stands too and touches my arm lightly. "You sure you're okay?" he asks, and I know he flirts with everyone, I know he's overly friendly, but I feel like there's something there in that touch, something real, something that connects me to him.

"I'm good, thanks."

"I guess I'll see you tomorrow?" he asks, another question lingering between us.

"Ya," I say. "French class."

And I expect him to walk away, but he doesn't. He's looking down at me, a sad smile on his lips. "Okay, well, I'll see ya," he says and I nod my head, unable to formulate the words that could possibly communicate my regret.

There's more he wants to say, but he's waiting for me. I had promised myself that I wouldn't keep my words down, that I would say them no matter what, but I'm powerless in this moment.

Levi nods and I let him walk away.

How to get Levi to forgive me

It should be raining
and he's going away somewhere
for an unknown length of time
and I have to chase after him
and catch him at the last minute
breathless and soaking wet
and he devours my apology as he
towels me dry

Or it should be the middle of the night
and I show up at his window
with a boom box or a song
and he rubs sleep from his eyes
not too surprised to see me
since I had appeared in his dream

Or I write him a poem
one with our metaphor
and when we are alone
I will say "here are my words
here is the gift of me
wrapped up in little versus
for you to unravel like a math problem
because, really, math and poetry
we are not all that different."

And he smiles, all teeth
wraps his laugh around my regrets
and forgives me

24

Not very long after I turn in my revised poem, I am relieved to see the red *A* on the top of my paper. I read Mrs. Skye's comments that include words like "insightful" and "brave." There's also a note at the bottom that says, *see me after class,* which doesn't sound good but it can't be bad, right?

"You wanted to see me?" I ask, holding my paper up.

"Oh, ya, I wanted to ask you something," she says, smiling. There's a little bit of sweat on her nose and forehead, an unfortunate effect of our unairconditioned school. "Hang on a second." As she's looking through some papers on her desk, she says, "Every year, I choose a few students from my classes and recommend them to this summer institute." She hands me a flyer. " It's for writers."

I look at the paper, trying to read the information there but my mind is buzzing. "Okay," I say, slowly, unsure of exactly what she's asking me.

"Well, it's held at a college in the city. So you'd

have to stay there for most of August. But, I really think that's you'd get in. It's a tough selection's committee, but I think, once they see some of your writing samples, you'd get in. And I'd write your recommendation of course."

She's looking at me intently but I can't speak. I watch a bead of sweat slide down her face.

"Wait, what?" I say.

"Your revised poem, Aster," she sighs, pretended to be frustrated, "and some of the other work that you've turned in recently, are really amazing. What do you think? Would you be interested in applying." Her voice is encouraging and alive.

"Ya," I manage, smiling. "That sounds awesome."

"I think this is a perfect opportunity for you, especially if you want to do writing in college. So talk to your parents about it and then we can work on the application together."

She hands me the application. I put it in my bag thinking I might be able to change the world.

*　　　*　　　*　　　*

That weekend, I sit at my desk, looking up the admission guidelines for the writing institute and read all of the sample poetry online from last year's students. I'm intimidated, that's for sure, but I'm also determined. If Mrs. Skye, whose poetry sings like wind chimes, thinks my writing is good enough, then it must be, at the very least, okay.

There's a soft knock at my door. "Can I come in?" Mom asks. She and I are talking for the most part, but every time we do it feels like we're both putting in a lot of effort to say the right thing.

"Ya," I stand up and open the door.

Mom's wearing gym clothes and her hair's spun into a tight bun. "Are you busy? I'm just heading out for a run, just seeing if you want to come."

"I actually ran this morning," I say.

"Oh, okay." She turns to go but I stop her.

"Actually, can I ask you something?"

"Of course," she smiles eagerly.

I walk over to my desk and retrieve the information that Mrs. Skye gave me and hand it to her. "I want to apply to this program. It's for writing and they have a specific workshop for poets. It's a little expensive though."

She barely glances at it. "Money's not an issue, you know that." She flips through some of the pages of my application. I've already attached some of my poems, but she doesn't look at those.

"Well, it's also a four week ordeal. So I'd be living there for a month."

"Oh," she says, looking more closely now. She sits down on my bed. "Is this really what you want to do?"

I thought I would lose my nerve when it came down to looking her in the eyes and just saying exactly what's on my mind, but I don't. "Yes," I say. "I'm sure. This is what I want to major in when I go to college."

Mom takes a deep breath and tries to smile, but I can tell it's taking a lot of effort. "It sounds great, Aster, really. I just think you need to think about your future. There's not a whole lot of money in writing. Just something to think about, okay?"

"I am thinking about that," I answer. "But I'm also thinking about being happy. I mean, are *you* happy?" I ask and I'm not trying to be fresh; I just don't know the answer. "You make all of this money, you live in this big house, you're in perfect shape, but are you happy?"

She smoothes out the papers in her hands, thinking. "I think so. Most of the time. Sure." But she doesn't sound sure at all.

"Did you ever want to do something that your parents didn't want you to do? Or be something they didn't want you to be?" I think about the poem she wrote all of those years ago. Did she ever dream that her words could change her world?

She laughs darkly. "Yes, Aster. *Everything.*"

"Really?"

"I've told you before. My parents never expected me to be anything but maybe a stay at home mom, like my own mother. When I told them I wanted to go to college, they dismissed it; paying for my college was a nuisance to them because I was a girl. They practically forced my younger brother to go even though he just wanted to fix cars," she says and sounds bitter. "It took me a marriage and a child to realize that I wanted more. And I worked really hard to defy my parent's wishes." She looks at me. "I guess that's why I push you to be something more. Because I don't want you to settle. I want you to know you can be anything. And you can have it all. You can change your life, just like I did."

"But Mom, I *do* want something more. Why do you see writing as something *less?"*

"I don't know," she says. "I guess I just thought you'd be more like me. I didn't want to raise you like my parents raised me. And Luke...you know...he's different from us. We're like the same person."

"That's the thing Mom. We're a lot alike, you're

right. But, we have different dreams. And, I don't look like you either. I will never be a size two. See these pictures all over my mirror? I've tried for years to become them, I really have, so that you'd be proud. But I'm just...it's not who I am. Can't you just love me for who I am?"

"I *do* love you," she says.

"I know. It's just that, sometimes, I'd think you'd love me more if...." but I can't get the words out, not if I have to contest with the frown on my mother's face.

But then she looks around at the pictures that cover my room and I think she starts to see. "You know I think you're beautiful, right?" she asks, dumbfounded.

My first thought is *no.* She has never told me this, not once. Not even when she dressed me up for that first dance with Adam, not even when I lost weight and dyed my hair the color she chose, not even when I put on clothes she bought for me. She maybe smiled at me, or smoothed my hair, or helped me zip up my dress. But she never once told me I was acceptable. And those words would have mattered.

Now, it's too late. Because she may want to be beautiful, and of course I do too, but I'm starting to release myself from its hold.
"I'm a lot of other things too, Mom."

"Of course you are," she says.

"And so why didn't you tell me that when Adam hurt me? Why did you tell me, in a really messed up way, that it was my fault...and that if I changed myself, I could get him back."

"I-I didn't. That's not what I meant. I didn't want you to get back together with Adam. I just wanted him to see you like I do."

"I wish you had just told me he was an asshole. Or a scumbag. Or trash. That would have made it a lot easier to say goodbye to him."

She is quiet, smoothing out the wrinkles on my bed. "I'm sorry," she finally says. "I thought I was helping you." She stands up and looks away from me. "I honestly don't know what anyone in this family wants anymore. It's like I can't make any of you happy." Her eyes are all of the sudden watery.

I uncross my arms, reaching out for her. "Mom, stop, you do-"

She steps back, puts her hand up to cut off my words. "Aster, enough. It's fine." She doesn't sound angry, just tired. She tries to smile again, but it only lasts a second. "If you want to write, go ahead and write."

"Okay, I will," I say.

She leaves my room, and I stay, forcing myself to be still and not run into the safety of her arms and beg for forgiveness.

When I come downstairs
later that night to get some water,
I'm thinking about how
I've never seen my mother cry

I've seen sadness
outline her face
but her eyes have always stayed dry
even at her father's funeral

My mother, if she mourned,
did so alone
preferring smiles and motion
to deflect any dangerous thoughts

Downstairs, all of the lights are off
but I can see a soft blare
coming from the living room.
Dad must have left the TV on again.

As I move towards the door to turn it off,
I stop. Both my mom and dad
are together in the semi-darkness.

Even though they are on opposites sides
of our smaller couch,
facing each other
they seem so close. I tiptoe
behind them to peek,
a spy in my own house

and the vision of them asleep
is the reason I'm so thankful

for poetry
so that I can capture this:

My mother in her silk bathrobe,
her mouth agape, snoring gently and
my father with her slender feet
tucked between his calloused hands.

{ SUMMER }

25

The last day of school is a half day and Leah and I have a tradition; we drive straight to the beach. We don't have a final exam for Mrs. Skye's class so she asks us instead to write letters of advice to our future selves, and she promises to give them back at this same time next year. This is what I write to myself:

Dear Aster,

You are worthy of love.

I know, no matter how many times I say it, my

cheeks still burn and I have to clench my teeth to keep from refuting the positive affirmation. Maybe when you read this in a year, it won't sound so distasteful and childish. Why is it always so hard to be kind to yourself?

Remember when you were young and you wanted, more than anything, to look like Mom? You were like her tail, always following a close step behind. It's taken you this year to realize that you can't compare yourself to her. You can't compare yourself to anyone. You should always continue to recognize the connections in this world, but you can't compare; it will surely rob you of any possible joy.

And make sure you visit Mrs. Skye and tell her often how much she has helped you, not only with your writing but with how you see yourself. Because words matter. She is the first person you envied not because of looks but because of intelligence and talent. She opened up this other world to you and showed you what it means to have self-compassion. Go easy on yourself, always.

Love, Star

"Hey Aster," Mollie says at the end of class. "You wanna hang out after school, maybe go get food or something."

"Actually, me and Leah are heading to the beach. You want to come?" I regret asking almost immediately, thinking about how it's just another person who will see me in a bathing suit, but I push the thought down, remind myself that I'm okay.

"Yes, definitely," she says, and I love how unafraid she is of meeting new people even after what happened with Max.

"I'll meet you outside, okay? I have to tell Mrs. Skye something."

Mrs. Skye is right outside the door, smiling and saying congratulations and good luck to all of us as we leave her classroom for the final time. I pretend I'm looking for something in my bag as I wait for all of the girls to leave.

"Aster," she says, stepping back into her classroom. "Any plans this summer?" She raises her eyebrows knowingly at me.

I smile. "I got in," I say.

She claps her hands together. "I know!" she says, not able to contain her excitement. "I got an email about it too. I'm *so* excited for you!"

"Thank you. For everything you did."

"It's been a pleasure." She stops to tidy up her desk. "So...how's it going with your mom?" she asks. That's the thing with poetry; it gives away the details of your personal life. "I know she was a little unsure about this."

"She's coming around," I say, glad that she asked. "When I told her I got in, she seemed happy or at least tried to be happy. It's so weird though because she used to write when she was younger. My dad showed me something she wrote. But she never told me, not even when I asked her about it indirectly. It's so annoying. Like, why wouldn't she be happy that we have this in common?"

"Hmmm. People are so complicated, aren't they? We never know why they do the things they do. That's why we are lucky to have poetry to read and write and help us explain and cope with the human experience."

Poetry as a survival tool. I had never looked at it that way. "Ya, I guess you're right."

"Just like with the books we love, not everything will ever feel neatly tied up, but I think you figured out a lot of things this year through your writing."

"Ya, almost everything."

"Well, good luck with your writing adventure this summer. Come back next year so I can hear all about it and read everything you wrote."

"Absolutely," I say.

*   *   *   *

I meet Mollie outside and we find Leah at her locker. I introduce them. "She's going to come with us," I say.

"Cool," Leah says.

As we leave the giant doors for the last time until next year, we run into Melody. She waves at us and comes over. "Hey," she says and I smile. I lean into her hug instead of avoiding it.

"Hey, we're heading to the beach," Leah says. "You want to come?" Another person to see me bare.

"Actually, I'm meeting up with Levi." She glances at me and I look down, relieved she said no but also his name, as always, makes my heart loud. I wonder if Melody can hear it. "I told him I'd drive him home. He has to wrap up doing some geeky math shit or something."

"No worries," Leah says.

"Maybe we'll meet up with you after?" Melody suggests. "I'll let Levi know that you're *all* going to be there." She looks pointedly at me again, not hiding anything. "Text me where you're at."

We all make our way to Leah's car and my mind is buzzing with fear and excitement and hope. Will Levi actually come? Do I want him to come to the beach of all places? Oh God, I cannot think of anything more terrifying and thrilling.

Mollie squeezes into the back seat and I take my familiar seat up front. I watch all of the other students leaving the doors of our school for the year, piling into each other's cars, smiling huge, grateful to have this summer. And then, my eyes, unable to help themselves, find Max. He's alone, leaning against his car, phone in hand. He looks up and then around the parking lot, like he's looking for someone. He looks angry or bored, I'm not sure. Eventually, his eyes find mine. I try not to look away. It doesn't matter; it's like he doesn't see me anyways because he's really looking at Leah. And I feel sad that in a way, just like with Trump's victory, Max won.

"What are you staring at?" Leah asks and I nod in Max's direction.

"Just Max," I say. "I want to punch him in that smug face."

"There's just no changing someone that ignorant," she says then stares back at him, smiles directly at him and then waves.

Max looks behind him and then back at us with a look of disgust.

Mollie laughs and then says, "God, that kid must feel all sorts of lonely."

"Why do you say that?" Leah asks.

"Aster, you know how I told you before that we both went to that group? Well, apparently his mom made him go because she thought he had a panic disorder. He lashed out at her all of the time, I guess, and didn't trust anyone. He played sports but didn't have many friends. He didn't make any friends in our group either. It just seems like he'll continue to project his unacceptable thoughts onto other people who are different from him which is, like, everyone. I think he hates feeling vulnerable and so he covers it up with, you know, being a complete asshole."

Leah raises her eyes at her. "Huh, I'm real glad to have a therapist as part of the group," she jokes.

"Hah, sorry. I've done a lot of healing, and part of that is analyzing other people's behavior."

Eventually, Max gets into his car. We drive away first, leaving him behind us, owing him nothing but our silence and our pity.

Beneath his confident ego

you will find
a creature of absolute paranoia
a stranger to kindness and love
a canvas without color

In front of your eyes
he is filled with rage
angry over your flaws
because it's easier
than coming to terms
with his own

that's why alone
he whimpers like a child
underneath a shaky sky

and we are able to carry on
away from storm clouds,
walk unafraid into the flawed arms
of another's pain and love

26

We drive to the beach and find a quiet spot. It's still early in the season, so the crowds will not yet descend and disturb our peace. We sit close to the water's edge, listening to the ocean. I'm wearing a black one piece bathing suit that shows off my strong shoulders and arms, and a bright blue cover up. Leah, Mollie and I build sandcastles and then kick cold water at each other, like children. We collect multi-colored rocks and skip smooth rocks. Later, we rest our wet, sand-speckled bodies on a large blanket and eat blueberries and sip lemonade, and I try not to think about Levi.

Leah rests her head in my lap and puts my hand over her eyes. "I forgot my glasses," she says. "Be my shade?"

"Is Melody coming?" I ask her, lifting my hand.

She squints at me. "Wouldn't you like to know," she says and smirks, putting my hand back over her eyes.

Soon more people gather on the beach. Leah and Mollie are both flat on their backs, sunbathing, looking sleepy and peaceful. Deciding that it's late into the day and doubtful that Levi will make an appearance, I finally take off my cover up and join them.

I rest my chin on my hands and watch the waves. I wish and wish and wish. But this time, I don't wish for thinness. I don't even wish to change myself. Because what I really want has nothing to do with being pretty.

Furtively, I watch a young woman spread her blanket next to us on the sand; she has a small girl in tow. The woman puts down her things and does not hesitate to strip off her sun dress to expose her very bright orange bikini and flabby belly that jiggles when she walks and rolls into dough when she sits to play with her child. This woman does not look around the beach to see who is watching; she does not fix or adjust her bathing suit; she only focuses on her little girl.

I want to live in her world.

I imagine that she will go home and lovingly cook dinner for her small family—maybe some pasta, definitely followed by chocolate cake. Her husband will put their daughter to bed early and, later that night, when the two retire to bed, he will savor her confidence, her sureness that allows her to take off all her clothes with the lights on. She does not feel the least bit shy when he lets his hands roam over her soft belly; she welcomes them.

This might not be the exact truth, but I hope that it is, for this woman and possibly, someday, for me.

Because even though I have envy and regret and longing in my heart, which I have had too many times before and will have many times again, I have begun to grasp at my fears by imagining this other life of bold weightlessness—a kind of possibility.

I think I doze off for a bit, but eventually wake up to someone yelling, "Hey!" Then I hear a familiar voice from behind us, "You bitches asleep?"

My heart is in a turbulent flutter as I sit up and see Melody. And beside her, this boy who is smiling down at me, all teeth.

"You're here," I say.

Levi does not hesitate and sits down right next to me, apparently not caring that the sand will stick all over his long legs. I don't mind the sand either.

"Hey, Asterisk," he says.

And even though his smile unburdens me with the promise that I am worthy, he is not here to save me.

"What's up?" he asks.

And following this simple question is a talk that lasts until the sun goes down and becomes barely a wink at the edge of the water. Our conversation is filled with all types of punctuation and laughter and sentences that we leave open for each other.
It's true that I have worried about my flaws for so many years, but these thoughts only softly tug at me

as his voice quiets any lingering dark thoughts.

Because Levi is every color.

Or maybe he *is* that black crayon: all of the primary colors combined.

And he is like that beautiful spell that poetry casts.

And me? I'm all hips. Just like the Nile, I take up space. I'm an ocean of words.

And I deserve him.

The Power of Words: Part II
By Aster Lamonte

This morning,
I am slowly peeling the women
from my mirror
thinking of my beautiful mother,
of her obsession with thinness,
hoping that my life
will be about something more

thinking about Hillary Clinton
who would have been the *first*
who could have changed a 100% statistic
and I'm disappointed
but I have glass of my own to shatter
and it might be as simple
as loving myself with my whole heart

After months of devouring poetry and art
of conversations and lessons and *words*
I am beginning to ease the war within me,
and suppress the demonic voices
of uncertainty
to see that I'm maybe okay
and understand that this thing I want so badly
is unattainable, like capturing air
or erasing things that were said

The trouble with all of us
was that we were battling
the piece of ourselves
that society rejected

with a learned shame
we tore ourselves apart
revealing our weak spots
like the first brown blemish
on a good piece of fruit
that would eventually make us rot

For me, it came down to size
believing I took up too much space
and that my body shape
might actually determine
the weight of my worth
how lazy I was in deciding my value
was just a number on a scale

For Melody, it came down to sexuality
believing what so many told her
that gay is a choice
for her, the only choice she made
was fully giving her heart to someone
who saw past her flirtations

For Leah, it was her pigment
that made her cool by default
but also an Other
in our small, white town
she had everything but
belonging

All this time
I had been seeing them as different
but we were all fighting
a similar demon

When the last picture
is gone from my mirror
there I am

I look exactly the same
but I feel
different

Point B
was here
the whole time:
I see it
in this stronger version
of myself

Tara A. Iacobucci

Acknowledgments

Kate Kelly, my devoted reader/editor/friend/ co-teacher. Thank you for our writing nights, for reading my book with so much love, and for your eager and hilarious comments on my google doc. Without you, this would have been a twenty page manuscript I once wrote for a college class. You made me realize that my dream of writing a book was an actual reality. Let's get started on our next ones soon, yes?

Joe Iacobucci, my husband/reader-by-duty. Thank you for letting me read you Aster's poetry even when it was past your bedtime. Aster's father and Levi exist in these pages because of you. I have had countless women who have inspired me to look at myself with love and compassion, but your words and consistent humor have been paramount to my growth. You don't speak much but when you do, despite what you may think, I *always* uphold your words, advice, and opinions. Thank you for loving me as is.

Mary Nee, CHS grad/my (former) school daughter/young reader. Thank you for taking the time to read my book and convincing me it doesn't suck. Your text came at a time when I really needed that reassurance.

Tammie Trucchi, my amazingly talented sister. Thank you for the beautiful cover art that so perfectly captured the theme of this book and for always inspiring me with each and every one of your drawings.

Nicky Cao, CHS student. Your photograph motivated me to write a few scenes in this novel and helped me to figure out a big piece of the plot. Thank you so much for letting me use it as the cover. I think you have a very bright future ahead of you.

407 poetry club, you know who you are. Wow. I just cannot believe how much talent exists in my classroom on Friday mornings. You have all been my motivation to write and finish this book, and I just hope the poetry inspires you all to keep writing. I am so proud of the risks you take with your poetry and the courage you have to read it out loud. (CC--thank you for letting me borrow one of your lines!) Kristen Morgan, I hope we will always have poets wandering into our rooms...thank you for our club.

My parents and my amazing friends who are family now. Thank you for letting me talk about my book, for watching my kids while I wrote, for wanting to actually read it. I could not ask for a more loving and supportive group of people to uplift me on a daily basis.

Dad, thank you for letting me/Aster's mom use one of your (very old) poems.

The Trouble with Pretty

Made in the USA
Middletown, DE
02 September 2017